Falling For The Heiress

A Hosta Falls Novel

Gabrielle Landi

Contents

To Mason, for always believing in me.

Could you give yourself a concussion by banging your head against the table? I was starting to wonder. It had been twenty minutes, and Mom was still going on about how overtired I was and how overworked I was and how she wished I would just take better care of myself, and banging my head into the table seemed like a good option at this point.

"Mom, I'll be okay," I said, looking at her pointedly when she paused to take a breath.

"I know you'll be okay," she said. "But you're still my baby and I worry about you."

"I'm not the baby."

"I know you're not." Mom laughed. "But you're all my babies, whether you're the youngest or not."

She was right though. I was overtired and overworked. But it was all going to be worth it when I finished my four years of college with no student debt. It hadn't been easy, but I'd managed it. And

I wasn't going to give up in the final semester. It was only three more months; of course I could handle that.

It might be difficult, but what wasn't? I'd gotten used to it, and I didn't have much longer to go before I would get my degree and a good job, settle down, and live the life I wanted. It was all coming together. I just had a few months left, and then I could start my future.

"I just worry about you, you know," she said again, oblivious to the fact that she'd already said the same thing about six hundred times.

"Mom. I'm fine," I said, letting the annoyance edge into my voice a little. "Can we just enjoy the rest of lunch without talking about it?"

She sighed and nodded. "Just promise me that you'll let us help if you need it."

"Of course, Mom." She did mean well, even if she didn't always show it in normal ways. I couldn't fault her for that, as much as I wanted to sometimes.

We finished our meals while talking about the weather, my siblings, and what project my dad was launching this weekend - something about building her yet another bookcase. When we called for the check, I fought her for it halfheartedly, knowing she wouldn't let me take it anyway, and grinned at her when she wrestled it away.

"I can't let you pay for this," I said.

Mom glared at me. "I'm the one who invited you out to lunch."

"I invited you."

She shrugged. "That's not how I remember it." Her eyes sparkled and she gave me a wink. "I can handle it. You work hard enough for five people, so the least I can do is buy you lunch occasionally."

"And let me live at home," I said.

"Yeah, well, we wouldn't be using your bedroom anyway."

I rolled my eyes. "I don't know, I bet Krystal would be happy to get her own room."

Mom laughed, pulling her wallet out and counting out cash for our meal. "For sure, but Krystal doesn't need to get everything that she wants."

With the check paid, we prepared to head our separate ways. I gave Mom a kiss on the cheek and held the door as we stepped into the parking lot. "Thanks for lunch, Mom."

"You're welcome," she said as she pulled me into a hug. "I love you, Keith."

"Love you too."

Mom waved as she pulled her purse over her shoulder and headed for her shop on the square. I slid into my car with a sigh, paired my phone to my car's Bluetooth, and pulled up my favorite sister's contact. We weren't supposed to have favorites, but as the sibling closest in age to me, Kaitlyn and I had always been closer than some of the others.

"How was lunch with Mom?" Kaitlyn asked as soon as she picked up the phone.

"It was lunch with Mom," I said, and she laughed.

"Sounds about right."

"You know, she just loves us too much," I said.

Kaitlyn agreed with no hint of sarcasm or hesitation in her voice. "She's the best mom ever. I do wish that she sermonized a little less sometimes, though."

She had a point. Mom was extremely good at going on and on about a topic, especially when it pertained to one of her children. She was so good at it, in fact, that all of us could probably give our own mom talk if we had to.

"So what do you have left this week?" Kaitlyn asked.

I took a look at my schedule on my mental calendar. "Hmm, let me think. Work, work, more work, school, homework in addition to the regular work, and probably more school."

"That sounds pretty familiar. You're working too hard."

I sighed and ran my hand through my hair. "I just sat through an hour of Mom telling me this. I don't need to hear it from both of you."

I could almost see her shrugging from wherever she was. "You know it's true."

"If it wasn't true, Mom wouldn't be telling me so much."

That was true too. No matter how much she drove us up the wall sometimes, we all knew Mom just wanted what was best for us.

"Well, Karen Palmer is not easily dissuaded," Kaitlyn said, "and if she can't get through to you, then I have no hope."

"Good, you can just go back to being my annoying little sister."

"I'm not annoying."

"Annoying is pretty much the definition of a little sister."

She snorted. "Yeah, tell me about it."

"They're my little sisters too."

"Yes, but you don't have to share a bedroom with them."

I laughed. "You don't either, anymore. We moved to the new house, what, eight years ago? And you share with Natalie now."

"I shared a room with them for years though," she said, "and I'm still scarred from the experience."

"Kathryn couldn't have been that bad."

"No, but Krystal was."

"Krystal hasn't been around that long."

"She was around long enough," Kaitlyn said darkly. "If I could go back and erase those years from my memory—"

"You wouldn't," I interjected. "You may talk a good game, but we all love Krys."

"Of course we do. Geez, what did you think I was saying? We still get to talk smack about her—it's in the older siblings' handbook."

"Ain't that the truth." I grinned as I turned into the work parking lot. "So what are you up to this week?"

"Just editing some family sessions I photographed last week, shooting a wedding this weekend, and probably hanging out with Natalie, too."

"When do you not hang out with Natalie?" I asked, pulling into my usual parking space and turning my car off. Ever since Kaitlyn's best friend had moved in with us, they spent even more time together.

"I mean, she's my best friend, I kinda like spending time with her."

I gasped in mock horror. "Wait a second, I thought I was your best friend."

"You're my brother, there's a difference. You might be my favorite but that doesn't mean you could take Natalie's place."

I would grant her that one. There was a big difference between a sibling and a best friend, though Kaitlyn somehow managed to be both my sister and one of my best friends. Not that I had time for many other friends—the friends I'd had through high school had all gone to fancier colleges than me and faded out of my life.

After watching my dad work hard all his life, and graduating high school knowing that there wasn't enough stored away to send all five of us Palmer kids to fancy colleges, I'd decided to work part-time to put myself through community college. I knew it would be hard, but looking back, it had been the right decision.

And I managed to luck into working in a great hotel in the downtown area of our closest city, which would hopefully help me get a great job with my hospitality management degree as soon as I graduated.

If everything went according to plan.

It wouldn't be long now. This final semester had barely started and it was already going quickly. Probably because of the sleep deprivation.

"Well, I've got to get," Kaitlyn said. "Don't get into too much trouble."

"Do I ever get into trouble?" I asked.

"Only constantly," she responded.

"Not as much trouble as you get into."

"That's not true," she protested. "I do not get into that much trouble."

"In your dreams."

"Well, there's not too much trouble you can get into, I guess, if you're just going to work."

"Yup," I said, "just another shift."

Not that I agreed with her—there was plenty of trouble I could get into at work, and none of it would be good—but so far I'd managed to avoid getting written up for anything, and I hoped to continue that trend.

Kait sighed. "You really do work too hard. At least you're proud of what you're doing... right?"

I smiled. Yes, I was proud of what I was doing. It was hard. It was exhausting. But fighting for my goals and dreams—and accomplishing them the way I wanted—was rewarding.

"And who knows," she added, not waiting for my response, "maybe one of these days you'll meet a hot chick at work, and it'll all be worth it."

I shook my head, even though she couldn't see me. "We're not supposed to talk to the guests, so it doesn't matter if they're hot or not."

"I didn't say she'd be a guest. Maybe you'll get a new front desk manager who's super hot."

I rolled my eyes. "Really?"

"What? Is it a crime to want my older brother to be happy?"

"Okay, look, just because you photograph weddings and adorable couples doesn't mean you need to set me up with every person you think would look cute with me."

A couple of coworkers walked past and I glanced at the clock on my dashboard. Just about time to wrap this up and head in.

"I'm not setting you up. I'm just saying, if you just so happened to get a cute new manager or something—"

And on that note.... "Goodbye, Kaitlyn."

She laughed. "Love you. I'll talk to you later. Be careful coming home."

"Love you too," I said automatically before hanging up and climbing out of my car.

Wouldn't it be nice if we did get a cute manager?

Not that I'd be able to do anything about it if there was someone cute, since I was too busy for a girlfriend anyway. But it never hurts having someone cute to work with.

Although, if I had to put up with my coworkers talking about the cute new manager, who was entirely hypothetical, fictional, and not at all real, maybe it wouldn't be worth it after all.

Great, Kaitlyn was getting in my head again.

By the time I'd clocked in, I'd managed to put all thoughts of fictional cute managers aside and was focused on thinking about the lecture that I'd listened to earlier in the day. I had a mixture of classes that enabled me to take various shifts at work, which was both good and bad since it entirely messed with my sleep schedule. On the plus side, I could pretty much sleep whenever now.

This particular evening, I was on from three to eleven, and I was already looking forward to getting to bed early-ish, hopefully by midnight.

When I made it to the front desk, uniform on, a smile firmly pasted into place, I found my coworkers all in a tizzy over something.

"What's going on?" I asked.

"The owner's coming in tonight," the front desk manager said, "so everyone's trying to make sure that everything is perfect for him and his daughter.

"Is there anything I can do?" I asked.

She grinned at me. "Just stand there and look pretty."

Despite her teasing words, the other bellhops and I were quickly pressed into service as a large wedding party arrived with more luggage than an army needed. It didn't slow down again until six o'clock, when a lot of our clientele were on their way to dinner rather than checking into the hotel.

"What time is the owner supposed to get here?" I asked as I came back from break.

"Probably any time now," the manager said. "And I'm assigning you to be their personal bellhop for the night."

"Whatever you want, boss," I said, offering a cheesy salute. "Do we know anything about them? Do they hate people who smile? Prefer silent or chatty?"

She laughed. "No, I don't know anything about them. All I know is they're here for the weekend, and I've been told that we're to do pretty much whatever they want, no matter the cost. Here, let me pull this up so you can identify them right away." She typed something into her browser and a picture of a stereotypical older white businessman popped up onto the screen. "This is Mr. Hanson, and this..." she typed something else and the screen loaded again, "is his daughter, Miss Sarah Hanson."

She clicked on one of the pictures that popped up and a candid shot of a laughing, smiling girl with dark hair filled the screen.

Well, it was a pity we weren't supposed to talk to the clients, because she was absolutely gorgeous.

Sarah

I was going to throw up soon.

The limo's AC was cold, but not cold enough to combat the motion sickness that threatened every time I got into the back of a car.

If it were up to me, we wouldn't get limos anymore, but some other type of vehicle, and I would be able to sit in the passenger seat. But image was everything when you were a Hanson. And that image included limos.

So every trip, every car ride, I sat in the back with the AC blasting, trying to keep my mind off my stomach, knowing that that wouldn't change anything but hoping desperately that it would.

Dad sat next to me, flipping through the important-looking paperwork that he never let me see. Even if I wanted to be, which I wasn't really sure I did, as a daughter I wasn't part of the business. I was simply a pawn in his games.

"What are you looking at?" I asked. Mostly to fill the air with something other than uncomfortable silence, since I knew he wouldn't tell me.

"Just some paperwork," he responded, barely even glancing at me. "Nothing important." Which was a lie, obviously, because he hadn't looked up from it the entire plane ride and the entire drive here.

At least we were almost at the hotel. It wasn't that far from the airport, unlike some of our other hotels. Hopefully once we got there, my stomach would settle before he brought up dinner.

I reached into my purse for some gum—something he would consider vulgar, but he wasn't paying attention to me anyway, and it was better than puking all over the limo. The sharp peppermint brought my mind away from the rolling of my stomach and helped settle it a little.

I had barely opened my mouth to ask him what his plans were this weekend when his phone rang. He glanced at me for half a second before answering, like he was considering if he could answer with me sitting there or not. I could hear the voice on the other end of the line, but I couldn't make out what they were saying.

Which was probably for the better, since no matter what it was, he clearly didn't care for me to hear it.

I leaned over and adjusted the air conditioning so that it blew more on my face and stared towards the front without blinking.

Almost there.

When we pulled into the parking lot, I sighed in relief. One more trip without puking. Hooray for me.

I waited for someone to open the door as every good society woman should, and let the driver help me out of the low-riding limo. The hotel's entrance had an overhang that saved us from the light drizzle that filled the cool twilight sky. It was barely fall, but it didn't ever get this cold at home, and my pencil skirt was scant protection from the chill.

Dad hung up the phone as he climbed out of the limo, ignoring the bellhop who rushed to get our luggage from the car.

"Let's go, Sarah," Dad barked, marching into the hotel, expecting me to follow without a word. I smiled at the driver who had opened the door for me and murmured my thanks before following Dad.

It wouldn't do to keep him waiting.

Since we were only here for a weekend, there were only two suitcases, so the bellhop quickly caught up. He followed us through the revolving doors to the front desk, where a manager quickly caught sight of us. She pasted a smile on her face, a practiced look that said she knew exactly who we were. "Hello, Mr. Hanson," she said, already pulling out a room key. "How are you this evening?"

Still on the phone, Dad ignored the manager entirely. Her smile faltered and she glanced at me. "We're doing well," I said with a smile, smoothing things over like a good Hanson woman. "Thank you. How are you this evening?"

"I'm also doing well," she said, holding out a room key to my father. "Your key to the penthouse, sir."

Dad swiped it from her hands and stalked away, not even bothering to nod. "Thank you," I said, the familiar twinge of embarrassment winding through my stomach, mixing with the nausea from the car.

"Here's a key for you, Miss Hanson," the manager said, offering me the second key. "And this is Keith. He'll be your personal bellhop for the evening. Please let me know if there's anything he can do to make your stay better."

I glanced over at the bellhop standing next to her. His dark hair was long on the top and short on the sides and his eyes sparkled as he gave me a real smile—unlike many of the smiles I was used to on these weekend trips with my father.

"Please let me know if I can be of any assistance," he said, his voice low and soothing. His easy grin made me feel right at home.

Surprisingly, the nausea had faded completely.

"Thank you." I smiled back at him. "I'm sure we'll be ordering dinner shortly, but until then, we'll just head to our rooms."

Keith came out from behind the counter and took our suitcases from the other bellhop, following us towards the elevator. My father stepped in and kept talking on the phone, waiting for Keith to press the button for the penthouse.

As we rode the elevator up the eighteen floors, I snuck a glance at Keith out of the corner of my eye. He was tall. Not so tall that many would notice, but taller than me and my heels.

When he caught me looking, he grinned before glancing back at my father with a solemn look.

That was what I was used to.

The elevator doors opened and Keith stepped out with our suitcases, his elbow brushing mine as he walked past. "Excuse me, Miss Hanson," he said, sticking his arm out to hold the elevator door for me. Then he walked quickly down the hallway with our bags, opening the penthouse doors and allowing us to walk in first.

I looked around the foyer, discovering which rooms configuration this hotel used. All of the hotels that our family owned used the same basic configurations. This was my favorite, the one where all three bedrooms had their own bathrooms with huge tubs.

I walked into the bedroom that I knew would be mine to set down my purse before walking back out into the common area. Dad was walking into his room, still on the phone. Without saying a word to Keith.

"Thank you," I said, knowing that my manners wouldn't make up for the lack of my father's.

"It's my job," Keith said, with a smile. "Can I get you anything else?"

I shook my head. "I think we're good for the moment. I'm assuming there's a menu in one of these drawers somewhere."

Keith walked over to the desk in the corner and pulled out the notebook that our hotels put together for their guests, holding it out to me. "There's a menu here, and a list of takeout. Just place your order and I'll be happy to bring you whatever it is."

I smiled and took it, pulling it to my chest like a shield. "Thank you, Keith."

"You're welcome, Miss Hanson," he said, nodding at me before he turned around and left the room.

I looked around the hotel room with a sigh, clutching the notebook. It was nothing new. I'd been in far too many of these hotels since I graduated college.

My humanities major and social standing gave me one purpose in our world, and that was being a trophy wife. Ever since I'd graduated, Dad had started bringing me with him on his work trips. Not so I could sightsee, but so that he could introduce me to his colleagues—and more importantly, their single sons.

Most of them were painfully single for a reason.

Which meant that unfortunately, there wasn't much interest on my side, but quite a lot on theirs.

I didn't want to deal with any of it, but as I'd been reminded a few times, this was my life. What I wanted didn't matter. Until I found a husband, Dad would be taking me around and showing me off and keeping me in the penthouse like it was a trophy case and I was something too precious to leave it.

If I didn't know it was all motivated by his pride, I would have found the thought endearing. But I'd learned long ago that my father only cared for me as a pawn in his game, and if I broke his rules again, there would be a penalty.

I opened the notebook and looked through the menus stashed there. A couple of the local restaurants looked good, but Dad wasn't a fan of takeout. If I couldn't order from his hotel's menu, well, clearly something was wrong with me because his hotels only served the best.

This hotel's menu was similar to every other hotel we owned. Each chef had their own specialties for their hotel, but most of the menu was the one that the Hanson group set out for them. My favorite pesto sandwich was there, so I already knew what I was going to order. I glanced at Dad's closed door. If he didn't come out in the next ten minutes, I would just order without him. But if I ordered right away, he would get cranky at me for not waiting.

I grabbed my bag and walked into my room. It wasn't really worth it to bother unpacking, but I pulled the packing cubes out of the bag anyway. Sometimes unpacking a little made it feel easier being in a different city every weekend.

Kicking off my heels, I grabbed the remote and looked to see what was on TV.

Nothing interesting, so I pulled out my phone and settled in to read the latest book I was inhaling.

Dad would scoff if he knew, but the romance novels that I hid in the Kindle app on my phone were sometimes my only escape.

There was a heavy knock at the door before it opened and Dad looked in without waiting for my answer. "Are you ready for dinner?"

"Yes, I am," I responded, sitting up.

"I already placed my order. Place yours." He closed the door behind himself, leaving me staring after him. Of course he'd placed his order without asking me. I shouldn't have expected anything different.

With a sigh, I took the phone off the bedside table, called for room service, and ordered my sandwich along with a couple of the sides.

I almost ordered dessert, but if Keith was going to be our personal bellhop for the evening, it wouldn't do to have him get bored. I could order dessert later when I was ready for it, and he could bring it up then.

Pathetic, Sarah. Making the bellhop work more so you can get another real smile.

With nothing to do, I went back to my book and lost myself in my imagination.

Before long, there was a knock on my door. "Come in," I said when it wasn't immediately opened. If it were Dad, he would just walk in, so it wasn't him. The door opened and Keith was there, which was surprising, but not unwelcome.

"I have your dinner, Miss Hanson."

"That was fast room service." I swung my feet off the bed together, careful to not let my skirt ride up.

"We take exceptional care of our guests," he said. That easy grin again. "Where would you like your food?"

"On the table out there is fine." I followed him out into the main room, watching as he rolled the cart to the table, setting down a selection of covered dishes, a pitcher of water, and two glasses.

"Can I get you anything else, Miss Hanson?"

I looked at the closed door to my father's bedroom.

I should tell him that the food was here, but sometimes it was easier to eat my own dinner before telling him. Then I didn't have to pretend everything was fine while he sat there and ignored me.

"Why don't you tell me about your city," I said, gesturing to the chair across from me.

He looked surprised, but sat down across from me. "What would you like to know about it?"

I shrugged. "I don't know, it's your city, not mine." I didn't get out much. I didn't even know what to ask about.

He thought about it for a minute, chewing on his bottom lip. "Well, we're known for baseball bats. We have a decent zoo, and there are caverns underneath it. There's a cool arms museum, if you're into history."

"I am into history," I said. "Tell me about that."

"Oh, I don't know anything about it." He chuckled, leaning forward to add, "But I bet I could get you tickets for tomorrow."

I shook my head. "No, I don't think I'll be able to go sightseeing this trip."

He looked genuinely surprised. "Are you sure? I could at least ask the concierge. Are your trips so busy that you can't go to a museum for a couple of hours?"

"No, no. It's not that. I just—I don't get out much on these trips. I tend to stay in the hotel."

Keith frowned, looking at the notebook on the table. "But if you like history, you should be able to go to the museum. Why travel if you're not going to get to see the sights?"

I sighed. "I know, I just—" I glanced over towards my dad's room. "My father prefers that I stay in the hotel."

Before he could respond, the bedroom door opened and my dad walked out, still on the phone. Keith stood quickly, the movement escaping my dad's notice as he stared into space, focused intently on his conversation. Keith pulled out the chair that he'd been sitting in, like he was simply pulling it out for my father, and took a step back and put his hand on his cart. "Can I get you anything else before I leave?"

"That will be all," Dad said, waving curtly as he walked over and settled into the chair.

Keith nodded, smiling at me from behind my father's back before turning and walking away, taking the cart with him. The penthouse door closed behind him and I found myself wishing that I was able to go with him.

"Okay, we'll see you tomorrow," Dad said before dropping his phone on the table, the sudden noise startling me. "That was one of my college friends. We'll be having brunch with him tomorrow."

I sighed internally. His college friend probably had a son my age who would just happen to tag along for brunch. "Of course. What time will we be leaving?"

This was my life. Being an heiress had many pros and many cons. The fact that I had little control over my life until I married someone my father approved of? Well, that was one of the biggest cons.

Keith

Climbing back into my car the next morning felt like torture. I'd gotten a mere six hours of sleep and had been called in for an extra shift because one of the other bellhops was sick.

It wasn't that I minded only getting six hours of sleep. I'd grown used to that.

But only getting six hours of sleep on the only day that I would be able to sleep in? That was the torture part.

When I got to work, I clocked in and headed for the front desk, where two of the other bellhops were waiting. Checkout wasn't until later, so we probably wouldn't have much to do until then, except sit around and talk and help the occasional elderly couple.

"I heard she's super hot," John said

"I looked her up before I got to work this morning," David said quietly. "Boy, she is smoking."

"Do I want to know who you're talking about?" I asked. It could be anyone from their latest celebrity crush to a girl they saw walking down the street, but I had a suspicion it wasn't either of those this morning.

"The owner's daughter who's staying in the penthouse," David said with a grin. "Think she'll come down later?"

"I wouldn't put it past her," John said, offering a high five.

They were right, she was smoking hot, and if they knew that I was here when she'd come in last night, they would start grilling me for details. But I felt oddly protective of her, in a way that I'd never felt when we discussed how cute the random girls who stayed in our hotel were.

Maybe it was because she'd actually talked to me for a couple of minutes? Or maybe it was because I felt sorry for her.

"I bet she's already taken anyway," John said.

"Even if she wasn't, what makes you think she'd go for you, idiot?" David asked.

"Well, I'm probably more handsome." John struck a power pose.

I rolled my eyes and walked away.

Like she would date a bellhop anyway.

She was a gorgeous heiress, and we were far beneath her on the social scale.

When Mr. Hanson and his daughter walked through the lobby on their way to what must have been a brunch, they were too busy arguing about who was helping the next car to notice. And when the owner and the heiress came back, David was on break and John was helping an elderly couple get into their taxi, so they missed them once again.

Miss Hanson caught my eye as she followed her father's brisk pace to the elevator and she smiled, oblivious to the fact that she'd been the topic of discussion the entire morning.

When her father left again a short time later, she didn't come down with him.

As we began to approach the end of our shift, the other bellhops were still talking about Miss Hanson. If she'd been a normal girl, she wouldn't have even crossed their minds after the leggy triplets walked through at ten in the morning. But apparently an heiress was worthy of more discussion.

I didn't engage since I didn't have anything I wanted to add to the conversation, and the manager at the front desk must have noticed that. Because when the lunch order from the penthouse came in, I was the one who he sent up with it.

The looks on John's and David's faces were worth every moment of having to keep my mouth shut.

Why was she ordering food such a short time after going out for brunch? It wasn't a ton of food, but still, she'd only gotten back two hours ago.

Maybe she just wanted to see a friendly face.

What did she do up in the penthouse when her father was gone? We hadn't seen her come down, and she told me she didn't go out.

She must get bored. Or lonely.

Why did she even come on these trips?

Were things worse at home?

Surely, her mother couldn't be worse than her father, who clearly didn't care for anyone.

When I reached the penthouse, I knocked and announced, "Room service." There was no answer, so after knocking and announcing myself again, I let myself in. "Hello," I called out as soon as I walked in and saw that the common area was empty. "Are you here?"

Once again, there was no answer, so I went to the room that I remembered as hers and knocked on that door.

Still no answer.

"Miss Hanson," I called as loudly as I could—hopefully without letting the other rooms below hear me.

They said the order was for the penthouse, right?

Had she snuck out without any of us seeing her?

When there was no answer, I opened the door and poked my head in a little bit, just to make sure no one was here before I took the food back down. She wasn't in the room. But there was a light on in the bathroom, and I thought I could hear a voice singing softly.

So that's where she was.

I backed out and closed the door quietly, setting the food on the table in the common area where she ate last night.

Should I wait for her or go? If it were anyone else, I probably would have left it.

But she seemed like she would be lonely. And after all, I should make sure that she was the person who had ordered the food. Right?

So I settled in to wait, picking up a couple of things that were out of place and putting them back. Even though that was house-keeping's job, not mine. If she didn't come out in five minutes, I would leave the food and go.

It was barely a couple of minutes before the door to her bedroom opened and Miss Sarah Hanson walked out in a T-shirt and shorts.

Nothing like the dressed-up, made-up heiress I'd seen the night before and this morning on her way out.

"Oh, hello," she said, her eyes bright and a wide smile on her face. "I didn't hear you come in."

"I knocked a couple times, but when there was no answer, I figured I'd set the food out."

"Well, thank you for not leaving with it," she said with a smile as she sat down at the table. "Are you hungry?"

I shook my head. "I'll be all right."

"Have you already had lunch?"

I hesitated long enough for her to guess the answer.

"So you must be hungry," she said. "Do you like cheeseburgers?"

"Who doesn't?" I asked.

"Well, why don't you join me."

It wasn't a request.

I sat in the chair across from her and she passed the burger over to me, taking the French fries for herself. "Were you going to eat all of this?"

She grinned. "I might have ordered a little extra just in case."

"Were you just going to invite whoever brought up the food to eat with you?"

She shrugged. "Probably not, but I didn't know. I didn't expect it would be you, though. I figured you would be sleeping."

"You thought I would be sleeping? This late in the day?"

"I know how late you were awake." She offered me the plate of fries and I took a couple.

The food here was pretty good, after all. It would be a shame to waste it.

"I don't get a whole lot of sleep," I said before shoving the fries into my mouth.

Her fingers tapped against the table. "How many hours did you sleep?"

"Barely six," I said, rounding up for her benefit.

"And that's enough sleep for you? I get grumpy if I don't get eight hours."

"I hope you manage to get those eight hours of sleep, then."

She laughed. "You'd be surprised how often I don't. There are quite a few charity functions that last well past midnight, with brunch the next morning."

"Yes, but at least it's not breakfast. Brunch could be as late as ten-thirty or eleven."

"True. It's usually enough that I can get more than six hours of sleep, thank goodness. You do not want to see me on less than six hours of sleep. I turn into a monster."

I widened my eyes dramatically. "Not a monster, oh no."

Her laughter made me grin as I took another bite of the cheeseburger. I probably wasn't supposed to be enjoying myself this much at work, but she'd brightened so much when she saw me that I couldn't convince myself to leave just yet. Besides, if I was talking to the owner's daughter, that counted as work. I wouldn't get in trouble for that. Right?

Ultimately, making the owner's daughter happy was worth more than potentially getting in trouble, right?

"So, tell me more about yourself," Miss Hanson said. "All I know is your name and that you don't get a lot of sleep."

I set the cheeseburger down. "There's not much more to it than that. I'm Keith Palmer. I go to school, and I work, and that's about all I do."

"It's nice to meet you, Keith Palmer. I'm Sarah Hanson. And I sit in hotel rooms and look pretty," she said with a self-deprecating smirk. But something told me that she wanted to do more than that. After our conversation the night before, I couldn't help but wonder... what exactly was stopping her?

"Well, I'm sure you are the loveliest thing this hotel room has seen in quite some time."

Her smile grew wider, and she shook her head at me. "I suppose I should assume you flirt with all of the patrons."

"Who, me? Flirting?"

"Yes, you," she said, the corners of her mouth turning up as she rearranged the plates in front of her. "I can tell."

"I would not risk my job by flirting with the patrons."

"There is that." She picked up a French fry and took a bite of it, staring at me while she chewed. "I have a question for you, Keith Palmer."

The way she said it instantly made me wary. I wasn't sure what to say in response, so I just raised my eyebrows, waiting for her to say what was on her mind. "Remember last night when we talked, and I said that my father doesn't like me to leave the hotel?" I still wasn't sure where this was going, but definitely not sure I liked the direction it was heading. "I was thinking about it all night. And I think you're right. I should be able to go out and see what I want. Don't you think so?"

This was dangerous ground. Either I agreed with the owner's daughter sitting in front of me or agreed with the owner. Someone who could potentially hear about this. And fire me. Probably blacklist me from his company, and he owned how many hotels? My hospitality management degree would only work so well if none of the hotels would hire me.

"I'm sure you could say that," I said diplomatically, but she let me get away with it, a coy smirk telling me that my reprieve would not last long.

"I would like to sneak out," she said, "and I want you to help me."

My eyes widened again, this time in surprise. "You want me to sneak you out?"

"Yes."

I shook my head. "I can't do that, Miss Hanson. I can't, I'm sorry."

"I thought you might say that," she said with a sigh.

"Why can't you just leave on your own?"

She looked away from me, her shoulders drooping. "I tried once before, and it did not end well."

She wouldn't meet my eye and I wondered what not ending well meant when you were an heiress and your father was one of the most powerful men in the country.

"So, I would need to wear a disguise this time and someone to help me get in and out."

"And someone to help take the blame?" I asked.

"No," she said strongly, turning back to face me. "No, no, I would never..." She trailed off, then shook her head again. "No. If we were caught, I would take the blame entirely myself."

"If you could," I said.

"If I could," she echoed, "I would take the blame myself. I just want to see something other than this hotel room. I understand if you can't help me. I really do. But if you change your mind, you know where to find me. I'll be here all day tomorrow, too." She looked down at her French fries, picking up two and shoving them in her mouth, still refusing to meet my eyes.

Would it really be that difficult to sneak her in and out?

I hated to see her looking so upset. Feeling dejected and broken down. As if my failure to help her meant she would never try again. I didn't want that. Didn't want my refusal to be the reason she gave up. Because she was right. She did deserve to get out and see things. She didn't deserve to be stuck in a hotel room constantly, however often she traveled with her father.

But how could I sneak her out without anyone noticing? The entire staff knew her face.

Plotting a way to sneak out an heiress is complicated.

There was so much at stake though. Was it worth risking it all for her? Was it worth losing my job, potentially being blacklisted? Having no way of getting an income to finish my final semester debt free?

I watched a single tear make its way down her cheek. She turned her head to try to hide it from me, but I knew instantly that she had won.

I was a Palmer man, and there were not many women who could cry without making me change my mind.

"You really want to do this?" I asked.

She took a moment to respond, wiping away the tear and swallowing hard. "I really do. You were right. I don't ever get to do anything. And I won't get to travel much for the rest of my life, so I want to be able to enjoy it while I can. I want to see interesting things, not just the inside of yet another Hanson hotel."

I looked deep into her eyes. "It's risky."

"I know it is."

"I don't know what's at stake for you, but I risk being fired. Or being blacklisted. Losing the only income I have while I work my way through school, in my final semester."

Her face brightened as she said, "I can help with that."

I waited for her to elaborate.

"How much do you need?" she asked. "How much would it take so you wouldn't have to worry about working this final semester... if something did happen?"

I pushed the now empty burger plate away from me and shrugged. "I don't know, it's hard to say."

"Would twenty thousand dollars do it?"

I couldn't help it—my jaw dropped.

Twenty thousand dollars?

"Just to be clear, you are offering me twenty thousand dollars to sneak you out, for what, exactly? An hour, two hours, a day?"

She shook her head. "A couple of hours while my father's gone. Relatively minimal risk. We just have to get past the front desk without anyone noticing me."

I laughed. "Every person down there has memorized your face in the last twenty-four hours. They'll notice you."

"I figured as much—that's what happened last time."

I thought about it for a moment. Twenty thousand dollars was a lot. She was right, it would cover me if the worst happened. If I got blacklisted, I would be able to travel somewhere, somewhere her father didn't have reach. That would be out of the country if

I wanted to work at almost any luxury hotels... but I didn't need a luxury hotel. I could make a nice living at a midline hotel.

I frowned at her. "You know this is something we shouldn't be doing, right?"

She looked up at me, a hopeful look crossing her face. "Does that mean we'll do it?"

I sighed. "Yes, Miss Hanson. I will help you. But we follow my rules."

She grinned. "I will do anything you ask."

Sarah

Waiting for Dad to leave was one of the hardest things I've ever done. Keith had promised to wait outside until five o'clock, then he was going to come back in and pretend that he'd left his wallet, which he probably had left just so he wouldn't be lying. He was going to use the excuse of meeting a friend at a bar just down the street to leave his car at the hotel without arousing suspicion.

He'd already apologized that we couldn't go to the arms museum, but since Dad wasn't leaving until dinnertime, the museum would already be closed.

I wasn't sure what we were going to do, but I was looking forward to getting out, to seeing the city, to doing something other than sitting in a hotel room.

And yeah, sure, I was a little nervous—the last time I'd tried to leave hadn't gone well. But with someone else to help me, as long as we were back at a reasonable time, it should all be fine. Dad never came back early on these trips.

In fact, I was usually in bed before he came back to the hotel room, so I knew we had at least until ten-thirty. I sat and watched the clock as I waited for Dad to leave for his dinner and drinks with a friend, time passing ridiculously slowly. It was probably the same friend who we'd met this morning. If I had to guess, they were probably discussing how to set me up with the son, Julian. As predicted, he had been entirely too interested in me, and not at all interesting himself.

Either way, it didn't matter. For the first time in a long time, I was excited to be here, and I couldn't wait to go out and explore the city.

At five o'clock sharp, my father left. He was nothing if not a man of habit. A few minutes later, there was a knock on the door and a bellhop I didn't recognize delivered me a package. "This is for you, Miss Hanson," he said, handing me the short squat box. "Can I get anything else for you?"

"That will be all, thank you." With the door safely closed, I opened the package to discover a baseball hat and a note. *Wear some of those ridiculously expensive sunglasses that you heiresses like to wear, this hat, a T-shirt and jeans, and no one will suspect anything*, the note read.

The plan was for Keith to distract the bellhops and front desk staff while I walked through the lobby, hiding in plain sight, wearing a disguise.

We would see how well it worked.

I was fairly confident though. Nobody ever saw me in anything other than a pencil skirt or other similar attire—jeans were not for Hanson women. So if I wore jeans and a T-shirt, those ridiculously large sunglasses, as he had called them more than once, and if I kept my head down and didn't look at anybody directly, there was a fairly good chance that no one would recognize me.

Once I made it out of the building, we had at least four hours until we had to think about coming back. Keith hadn't told me what we were going to do yet, but I was fairly confident that I would enjoy anything that involved not being in the hotel room.

I was already wearing my jeans and a T-shirt since those were my go-to when I wasn't out with my father or on official business. But thinking back to the bellhop who had just delivered the package, I decided to change before heading down. I grabbed a different shirt, changed into comfier shoes, and made my way to the elevator.

This was the tricky part. No one else was on this floor, so if anybody noticed that I was coming from the penthouse, they would recognize me.

Hopefully no one would be on the elevator until at least three or four floors down, away from the penthouse. Hopefully no one would get on the elevator at all, because it was close quarters for the entire ride and anyone who joined me might recognize me.

The elevator made it safely down to the fifth floor before anybody got on, and it was a young couple too wrapped up in each other to notice me.

When we made it to the ground floor, the elevator doors opened and I strode through the lobby, not making eye contact with anyone, walking confidently as if I belonged there. Like I was supposed to be making my way through the lobby without anyone to chaperone me. I didn't look over at the desk. Didn't look to see if Keith was holding up his end of the bargain.

I just walked.

A few moments that felt like an eternity later, I was out the doors, and a few moments after that, I was down the sidewalk, away from the prying eyes of anyone who should suspect me of being linked to the hotel.

Keith had told me to walk a block to the left and wait for him at the light.

It wasn't long before I heard footsteps behind me and I chanced a look to make sure it was him and not some random stranger.

... Though, to be fair, Keith was also a random stranger, just one I'd met slightly longer ago.

It was him, grinning as he caught up to me quickly, his legs longer than mine.

"Nobody suspected a thing," he said.

I could hardly contain my smile. I was out. I was free. And I was going to enjoy myself.

"We did it," I said, giving in to the urge to grin. I wanted to shout, spin in a circle, hug him—no, not that last one. Not appropriate.

"Thank you, Keith."

"Don't thank me just yet—we still don't know what we're gonna do."

I laughed. "I'm out of the hotel room, I don't care. What do you think we should do?"

He thought about it, then cocked his head, looking at me. "Have you ever been country dancing?"

I raised an eyebrow. "You mean, like, line dancing?"

"Yeah, line dancing. Have you ever been?"

"Where do you think I would ever have the chance to line dance?"

Keith shrugged. "You never know. Maybe they teach line dancing in Heiress Prep School."

Wouldn't that be a sight to see? I laughed at the thought. "Heiress Prep School? Don't believe everything you see on TV. Even if I went to Heiress Prep School, they wouldn't teach line dancing."

"Would you be interested in it?" he asked.

I thought about it for a second. It did sound interesting. I was a decent dancer and could probably pick up the steps pretty quickly without embarrassing myself too badly. "I could be persuaded."

"Then how about a bar and country line dancing? McGuire's right there is a fun place. Unless alcohol isn't your thing, which, no shame in that."

I looked across the street at the bar. "Now you're talking," I said with a grin. "But I need you to promise to remind me not to have more than two drinks. I get a little tipsy after that, and my dad would notice right away."

"No more than two drinks, got it," he said, gesturing to the crosswalk to our right. "Lead the way, Miss Hanson."

I may not get very many nights of freedom, but this was shaping up to be a pretty good one.

"McGuire's doesn't sound like a country bar," I said, turning to face him as the light turned and I started to cross. "How did you hear about it?"

He opened his mouth to respond, then turned pale and lunged for me, shouting my first name. He grabbed my arm and pulled me into him, crushing me in his arms as a car shot past, the breeze blowing through my hair. A car, driving full speed through a red light, through the space where I'd been half a second earlier.

I stopped breathing as I registered what had just happened.

What the hell.

"Are you okay?" he asked, still holding me in his arms. Like he was scared I'd bolt into traffic if he let me go. "Miss Hanson? Sarah? You've got to breathe, please start breathing."

At the reminder, I started breathing again, my mind racing to catch up to what had just happened, suddenly aware that I'd almost died a second ago.

"You saved me," I said.

He nodded, not smiling, looking at me like he thought I might break. "Of course I did."

My heart was beating faster and I was having trouble breathing again. "I almost died."

"But you didn't," he said lightly. "I wouldn't have let you."

As my adrenaline spiked, I started shaking and Keith took two steps backwards to pull us out of the road and back onto the sidewalk.

"It's okay," he said, beginning to rub slow circles on my back. "You're okay."

When my breathing sped up again, he counted breaths for me, keeping me from panicking any more than I already was.

I collapsed into him, resting my head on his shoulder and trying to focus on breathing.

I'd almost died.

That car had run a red light, and it had almost hit me.

Would've killed me.

If Keith hadn't saved me.

"I've got you," he said, "you're okay, we made it."

He had me.

I was okay.

We made it.

One.

Two.

Three.

In.

Out.

In.

Out.

People brushed against me as they walked around us. I listened as cars drove past, the sound bringing me back to the moment. And as I came back down from my panic attack, I noticed just how good Keith smelled. Like apple pie and brandy and other spicy comforting things.

I took a deeper breath, the smell grounding me.

Keith waited patiently, murmuring breath counts in my ear every time my breathing changed.

I had no idea how long it was before I stopped shaking and lifted my head from his shoulder, where I noticed a damp spot on his shirt.

I hadn't realized I was crying.

"You good?" he asked quietly.

"I think I'm good." My voice was still a little shaky. "Thank you."

His hand stopped rubbing slow circles on my back. I didn't want it to stop. "Don't mention it."

"No, seriously, thank you for saving my life."

"What did I just say?" he asked, turning a little red. "It's all good."

As the adrenaline faded, mortification took its place. "Sorry you, uh, had to see that." I'd had panic attacks like this before, but the only people I'd ever been around during one were my parents, and they were not so understanding. More than once, Dad had told me to get over it if I showed even the slightest possibility of panicking around him. Hanson women didn't do that—not that Hanson men did either. But it was very obvious that he would never deign to have a panic attack himself.

Having a panic attack in front of someone I'd barely just met, who not only didn't immediately shut down my emotions but helped me through it?

That was a first.

And as embarrassed as I was, I couldn't help but wonder if that was how other families dealt with crap like this. With compassion and care and sympathy, instead of derision and scorn?

Did he have experience with panic attacks? Because it certainly seemed like he did.

"You ready to go?" Keith asked after a moment.

I let go of him and took a step back, attempting to regain my composure and my pride. "Yeah, I'm good," I said. "I'll just look a little more carefully before I cross the street."

"That seems like a smart decision."

After the crosswalk sign changed to "walk," we made our way across the street together. Keith waited for me to make the first move, then followed me protectively, his hand hovering above my elbow as if he was ready to yank me back to safety again at a moment's notice.

When we reached the other side, I paused outside the bar to take a deep breath in anticipation. "I'm not sure that I've ever been in a real bar. I never really had the chance or wanted to go to one."

Keith smiled as he opened the door for me and gestured for me to go first. "Well, I'm glad to be the first to introduce you to one. This place is one of my brother's favorites, and one of the only ones I've been to. We don't come down here very often, but when we do, it always shows us a good time."

"'We'?" I asked, pausing in the doorway. "A girlfriend?"

I should've thought about that before I let him hold me through a panic attack.

He laughed. "No, no girlfriend. I'm too busy for that. My brother brought me down here to celebrate my twenty-first birthday, and I've come with him and his girlfriend a few times."

"How many siblings do you have? Just the brother?"

"I also have three sisters," he said. "They're all trouble."

He sounded so affectionate, even as he claimed his sisters were trouble. "I don't have any siblings. It must be fun to have so many."

We stepped into the bar, which was loud, chaotic, a little dark, and smelled amazingly strange.

"Can I get you a drink?" Keith asked.

"Oh no, let me get it," I said, pulling my wallet out of my purse. "What do you want?"

He shrugged. "Whatever beer they have. If they have a Yuengling, maybe?"

"Coming right up," I said, threading my way through the crowd to the bar. Keith followed, still hovering protectively over me. How much of it was him watching over me because he wanted to and how much of it was because he was afraid of losing his job if anything happened to me?

"A Yuengling and a margarita," I said when I reached the bar, like I'd seen people do in the movies. The bartender nodded, and a few moments later, we had our drinks and were making our way to one of the tables along the dance floor.

"We're gonna get you drunk, and then we're gonna go dance," Keith said with a grin as we sat at a table for two.

"No," I protested, and he laughed.

"I was kidding about the drunk part. Two drinks. I remember."

"I was serious about that." We almost had to shout to be heard across the music.

"Are you going to lose your head and forget about your limit after the first one?" he asked.

"Not likely. However, I am going to need some food or this is going to go straight to my head. I'm assuming they serve something here?"

His eyes swept the room before settling on something by the bar. "Yes, they should serve something here. Let me see if I can find a menu for you."

He stood and left, and I looked around the bar. There weren't many opportunities for me to go out drinking at home, and even if I could have at college, there hadn't been anyone I really wanted to go out drinking with. And since Dad never let me out of the hotel room unsupervised, I'd never been to one while we were traveling.

Maybe a hotel bar, but not a bar like this.

It was dark, the music was loud, there were people everywhere, and it was heavenly.

Keith returned with a menu and we ordered some food. Even though I wasn't that hungry, I knew I needed to eat before I drank too much. I'd had enough experience with alcohol at home to know that it did not mix well with an empty stomach for me.

I didn't plan on drinking too much. There was no need for it. Especially since I was out with someone who technically was still a stranger.

Yes, I'd known him since yesterday. But other than his name, the fact that he had four siblings, and that he worked at my father's hotel, I didn't know anything about him.

And that was less than ideal.

My father would kill me if he knew that I was here right now, alone, in a bar, grabbing drinks with a guy he'd never met.

Well, technically he *had* met Keith. He just hadn't paid any attention to him.

I cracked a smile at the thought of my father discovering that I had snuck out to a bar—and then prayed that it would never happen.

Because if it did happen, I would probably be grounded for life.

Though as the drink gave me a buzz, I wondered if being grounded for life might be worth it.

"Are you ready to dance?" Keith asked.

"I don't know," I said, looking over at the dance floor full of people line dancing to a country song I didn't know. "We may go out there and look like a couple of fools."

"That's entirely possible."

"But you know what? I won't mind looking like a fool right now. Because I'm out enjoying myself, and it's not like anyone will recognize me, and it's probably good for me to feel like a fool occasionally."

"My mother would agree with you," Keith said, holding up his drink. "Cheers to that."

A basket of onion rings and another of mozzarella sticks arrived and I grinned. "Greasy fried food. Perfect."

"You probably don't get this too often, do you?" Keith asked.

"No, I'm more likely to get fancy French food."

"I don't suppose French fries count?"

I laughed. "No, no they do not."

We finished our first drinks and the rest of our food. Keith sat down his now-empty glass and looked at me. "Ready?"

I shook my head. Suddenly, trying line dancing for the first time seemed so much more intimidating. I swallowed the last sip of my margarita—not that it was more than a drop—and sighed. "Not really, but let's do it anyway."

"A rousing endorsement," Keith said, pulling out my chair and leading me to the dance floor. "If you don't have fun, we can leave, I promise."

We were met with a crowd of enthusiastic people who pulled us into their ranks, a helpful woman on my left calling out the steps to us as we laughed and bumped into each other and turned the wrong way and bumped into other people, having the time of our lives the whole time.

At least five songs later, laughing and out of breath, I grabbed Keith's hand and dragged him off the dance floor. "I'm so bad at this," I said, sagging against the closest railing.

"I don't know, you're not any worse than I am," Keith panted, leaning against it too. "Geez, I should not be this out of shape."

I looked up at him and maybe it was the margarita, maybe it was the laughter and the heat getting to me, or maybe it was the way he'd taken care of me during my panic attack, but everything in me was pulled towards him, wanting to wrap my arms around him. I looked away instead, taking deep breaths, a self-conscious giggle bubbling up in my throat.

Where did that come from?

"You want another drink?" Keith asked, pushing off the railing and gesturing towards me. "Come on, let's find a seat."

His hand was still stretched in my direction so on impulse I took it, letting him lead me away from the dance floor.

When he spotted an empty table, Keith deposited me in a chair, pulling it out for me and pushing it in like a gentleman. "I'll be right back with our drinks—you want another margarita, or something else?"

I thought for half a second, then shrugged. "Surprise me."

He walked away, brushing past full tables on his way to the bar. I looked out at the dance floor, which was packed with people—had we managed to snag the only empty table?

"Hey there, pretty thing," a voice slurred over my shoulder as someone jostled me from behind. "You're too sweet to be here alone." A large body dropped into the empty chair next to me, another one brushing against my other side. My heart started beating faster as someone I didn't know invaded my personal space. "What's your name?"

"I'm not alone—" I began, and he laughed.

"Oh yeah, fake boyfriend? I got you. Don't worry, we can handle him," the inebriated young man in front of me said. His forearms rested against the table, an open beer in one hand. "You go to school around here?"

His buddy behind me moved closer, bumping my chair, and my heart rate skyrocketed. "I have a boyfriend."

"Like I said, sweetheart, we can handle ourselves, and we'll take care of you too." He set down the empty beer and reached out to grab my shoulder.

"Don't touch her."

I'd never been more relieved to hear anyone's voice in my life. I looked up to see Keith coming in fast, shoving the last two people out of his way to get to me faster.

"Dude, she wasn't joking," the drunk sidekick on my other side said.

"Yo, we didn't mean anything," the jerk in front of me said as an angry Keith towered over him.

"Get out of here," Keith said, his voice low and menacing. "Don't touch her, or any other girls. Just get out."

The dude scrambled out of the seat and he and his buddy disappeared quickly. Keith dropped into the now vacant chair, slowly reaching out for my hands, giving me the chance to pull away. "You okay?"

I didn't realize my hands were shaking until they stilled in his grasp.

"Does this happen every time people leave their homes?" I asked wryly. "First I nearly die, now this?"

Keith grinned, his thumb slowly stroking my skin. "No, this isn't normal. I guess it's just because you're special. I do feel bad, though, that this is all happening." He waited a moment until I was breathing normally before asking, "Are you ready to go home?"

"I think I am," I admitted, getting to my feet. "This has been a fun adventure, but I think I have had enough adventure for one night."

Keith stood, pulled my chair back, and offered his arm. I took it and let him guide me through the crowded bar and out into the cool evening air. When we were within sight of the hotel, Keith dropped his arm and I immediately missed his warmth as he pulled away. "Ready to get back to reality?" he asked.

I looked up at the hotel and sighed. "Not really, but I don't think I have a choice. Thank you for tonight."

"You're welcome," he said, grabbing the baseball cap on my head and tugging it down to hide my face a little more. "I'll go first and distract the front desk. Let me know when you make it up safely, please."

He walked away, shoving his hands into his pockets. Why did it feel weird to watch him walk away?

He'd given me the best night of my life—maybe that was why?

And it had only cost me twenty thousand dollars.

"Hey, wait a sec," I called, jogging a little to catch up to him. "Forgot to write your check." He opened his mouth and I shook my head. "If you're gonna say no, don't bother. I appreciate everything you did for me tonight and the adventure that we've had. It meant a lot, how well you took care of me. So you're getting it, whether you want it or not."

He took a deep breath, but closed his mouth. I nodded in approval as I pulled my checkbook out of my purse and quickly wrote a check for twenty thousand dollars.

Since it was coming out of the non-Dad-approved checking account that Mom had helped me set up, Dad wouldn't know any better.

Which was important, because if Dad saw a charge for twenty thousand dollars, I would have a lot of explaining to do.

It would take a significant chunk of my hidden fund, but it was worth it for a night of freedom.

"Thank you for tonight," I said, putting the check in his hand.

"You're welcome, Miss Hanson."

He had returned to his bellhop persona. I could see it in his eyes, stiff, unyielding, and polite to a fault.

I didn't like it.

"You know, I really don't mind if you call me Sarah."

Keith looked around and shook his head. "Not within hearing of the hotel. But let me know if you want to do this again next time you come to town—and you wouldn't have to pay me."

I grinned. "I would love that. Why don't I get your phone number and I can let you know next time I'm coming in?" I pulled out my phone, opened a new contact, and Keith rattled off his number, watching me put it in. "Thank you for the adventure," I said one last time. "It meant a lot to me to be able to go out and see things."

"Even with almost dying?" Keith asked, sliding the check into his back pocket.

"Even with almost dying," I said, flinging my purse back over my shoulder. "I would prefer not to repeat that part, though."

"Yeah, I would prefer not to repeat that either." Keith shoved his hands into his pockets. "I can see the headline now. 'Innocent Bellhop in Prison for Murder After Heiress Run Over in Crosswalk.'"

"I wouldn't let them do that to you," I said.

"You would be dead," he pointed out.

"Oh, yeah." I grinned. "Yeah, my father would definitely have you in prison."

Keith grimaced. "That's my point. Are you sure you want to do this again?"

I chewed on my bottom lip, not sure if I should admit just how much I wanted to do this again. "I don't know if we'll be back anytime soon."

He paused. "Well, if you want to do it again, let me know." He shrugged. "A little danger every once in a while is good for me. Now, I'll distract them, you sneak up, and let me know once you're safely in your room without your dad finding out. Thank you for a fun evening, and if I don't get a chance to tell you later, it was nice meeting you."

He walked away before I could echo the sentiment. It had been nice meeting him. More than nice. It had been wonderful.

I waited until he entered the hotel to follow, striding through the lobby with my sunglasses and my hat. No one even looked at me, but I waited until I got into the empty elevator to grin from ear to ear.

That had been one of the best nights I'd ever had. Even with the almost dying and the panic attack and the douchebags and the fear of discovery.

When I made it to the penthouse safely and into my room without a single sign of Dad being back, I quickly changed into pajamas and climbed into bed with a sigh of satisfaction.

I pulled out my phone and pulled up Keith's contact. *Thank you for tonight.*

Best night ever.

October

Keith

It had been a month since my evening with the heiress, and that twenty thousand dollars had changed my life.

I was still working, but only a couple of shifts when I wanted to so that I would still be around if she ever came back. Not that I thought I would get another twenty thousand or anything—I wouldn't take it even if she tried—but because that evening had been fun and I wanted to do it again. I wanted her to be able to do it again. And I doubted she would do it with someone else.

I hadn't had that much fun with anyone in ages, and the thought of doing it again... well, it was the reason I still worked one or two shifts a week.

So when I got there for my Thursday evening shift, I was pleasantly surprised to hear the whispering among the staff that meant something was going on. And I wasn't going to admit it to anyone, but I was hoping that it meant Sarah Hanson was coming back.

"Did you hear, dude?" Brian asked, smacking me on the shoulder.

"Hear what?" I asked.

Brian looked around to make sure no one was listening. "The owner is coming back. I guess he liked it last time he came through."

"Or he just has meetings here," David said, rolling his eyes as he fixed his glasses. "What are you thinking, he liked your service so much that he's coming back just for you?"

"Well, he can have meetings and like it here too," Brian defended himself.

I tried to contain my smile. If Mr. Hanson was coming back, maybe Sarah would be coming with him. Maybe she'd want to sneak out again. Maybe she'd ask me to take her.

"When are they coming back?" I asked.

"I heard they'll be here tomorrow," Brian said. "Then we might get to see the heiress up close."

"Man, I didn't see her at all last time she was here," David said.

Had she texted me? I'd thought maybe she'd want to sneak out again, but maybe she'd changed her mind. Maybe her father had found out and she'd gotten in trouble.

It didn't matter if she didn't want to sneak out again. Right? It wasn't that important. I wasn't that important. The little thrill that happened every time I thought about her didn't amount to anything, because she was an heiress and I was just Keith Palmer, hotel staff.

It didn't matter.

But as much as I told myself that, I couldn't wait until my break when I could check my phone for a text.

And there it was.

Hey Keith, I'm coming back into town and I was wondering if you will be around this weekend.

Just a simple text, and yet, my heart was racing.

Yeah, that would be great. Same timing?

If I had to rearrange my entire schedule or trade shifts with every bellhop who worked here, it would be worth it.

The question was, should I be working or not working?

If I was working, I'd be here and get to see her, but I wouldn't be able to get away with her.

So I probably shouldn't work Saturday evening.

Maybe?

I stared at my phone for my entire break, but she didn't answer.

I rearranged a couple of shifts, based on the best guess I had, so that I would be working Friday evening and the Saturday morning, ending at three o'clock in the afternoon, which would give me time to prepare to take her somewhere after her father left for dinner Saturday evening.

Hopefully that would work for her, because it was going to be a pain to undo. Brian was stoked to have Friday evening free and David was excited to sleep in on Saturday morning.

"Why are you working so much this weekend, dude?" David asked. "I thought you were done working so much."

"He probably just wants to see the heiress," Brian said.

I shrugged. "Well, I've got a surprise for my mom coming up this week that I have to pay for, and I have a friend coming in Saturday evening who I want to spend time with. Therefore, two shifts in a row."

Technically I had been planning on surprising my mom with flowers in the next week or two, so it wasn't a lie.

"When do you even sleep?" David asked.

I grimaced. "I don't."

It wasn't particularly true. I'd slept a lot more since getting that twenty thousand from Sarah. But it hadn't been that long since I'd gone on no sleep, and it was easy enough to conjure up memories of that time.

Brian came back from helping a woman with her suitcase and fist bumped David. "We're totally gonna get to see the heiress this time, though."

I sighed. Back on this topic again. Was it ever going to end?

"She's so hot though. How did we miss her last time?"

While my annoyance levels rose with their repeated mentions of how hot she was, I grinned at the reminder of how easily I snuck her out simply by putting her in clothes that no one expected her to be in.

Maybe I should bring an extra hoodie this time, just for an extra layer of disguise. No one batted an eye at a girl wearing a local college hoodie.

"Maybe she just didn't leave," Brian said.

"She had to leave at some point. Like she spent the entire time in the hotel." David laughed. "She was probably at a spa or something."

Little did they know, she actually had spent most of the time in our hotel.

What did she do when she wasn't on trips with her father?

"Maybe she's got a super hot boyfriend and they spend lots of time doing super hot things,'" Brian said.

"In the hotel suite?" David asked.

"No, I mean normally, when she's not here."

I tried not to grind my teeth as they continued to talk about what they imagined Sarah did during her normal day-to-day life. I didn't know what she did, but I knew well enough to know that what they were thinking wasn't it.

When the conversation started wandering to more lewd topics, I'd finally had enough. "Maybe we should stop talking about her. If you don't watch it, the constant objectifying is gonna get somebody fired."

Brian's eyes widened. "You really think so?"

"You think the managers don't know what you're talking about?" I asked.

He whipped his head around to look at the front desk, where one of the managers was helping a clerk check in the client David was helping. "Oh man, they do. Every time I mentioned, you know, I could feel them staring at me."

It wouldn't hurt to put the fear into him. "I wouldn't talk about her anymore if I were you."

It was almost comical how quickly he shut up after that. A few minutes later, he whispered, "Dude, do you think any of us are going to get in trouble?"

"No," I said with a shrug, "but probably best not to tempt it."

Better for my sanity, too. I could only listen to so much of the conversation when I knew the girl they were talking about, and that she wouldn't like it.

After a long and restless shift, I drove to the coffee shop to get some homework done before I went home.

I was maybe twenty minutes into homework when I got a phone call from Kaitlyn.

"Where are you?" she asked, without saying hello.

"I'm at the coffee shop," I said.

"Okay, I'll be there in a couple minutes."

It wasn't like her to not say much. What was going on?

When Kaitlyn arrived a few moments later, she pulled out the seat across from me.

"What's wrong?" I asked as she melted into the chair, leaning her head against the table. "You okay?"

"I don't know what I'm doing," she said miserably, refusing to look up at me. "Every time I think I've got things figured out, everything goes wrong again."

Because my sister always had to feel like she was in control, discovering that adulting meant not having any control had been rough. "Unfortunately, life is like that sometimes," I said.

"You're not helping," she wailed quietly. "You're supposed to help."

"Mom's supposed to help," I said. "Big brothers aren't supposed to actually help. We're just supposed to torture and tease until it's time to intimidate the boyfriend—then we can help."

"Intimidating isn't helping," she said, lifting her head to roll her eyes at me. "That's fun for you."

Well duh. That was the reason we did it. I grinned at her. "I know it is. So when are you going to let me do that? Hmm?"

She shrugged. "I haven't found anyone worth it yet, so why bother."

That's not what I'd overheard Kathryn and Krystal whispering about the other night. "I thought I heard somebody was asking you out."

Kait grimaced. "How did you hear about that? And yeah, but he's an idiot. So I said no."

"Oh, my little sister is a dream crusher, I see."

"Yeah, I felt kinda bad. I think he cried."

"Good for you."

She dropped her head onto her arms again. "I didn't like doing it, you know."

"That's why I said, 'Good for you.' I know it's not easy, but it's better to let him down now than to lead him on because you're afraid of telling him no." I reached over to pat her arm. "You've got this."

"There's another guy," she admitted. "This one might actually be worth dating, I don't know, but every time I think he's actually going to ask me out, he turns cold again. Why is it so confusing?"

"I mean, I'm down to intimidate non-boyfriends too," I said, poking her shoulder. "You just let me know the time and place. And I'm not sure what exactly you're failing at, but whatever it is, I know you. You won't fail at it for very long."

Kaitlyn lifted her head and smiled at me. "Thank you. I guess I just needed someone to tell me I wasn't being foolish."

"Oh, you're probably being foolish," I said.

"Hey," she protested.

"What? I have to be honest."

Kaitlyn rolled her eyes and stood up. "Do you want anything?" I shook my head, taking a sip of the water bottle I'd bought, and went back to studying. When she came back though, there were two drinks in her hands and one of them appeared in front of me.

"I said I didn't want anything."

"You need the caffeine. Drink it."

I picked it up and took a sip, not at all surprised that she'd remembered that I liked cappuccinos with just a hint of flavor. She was good like that.

"So, how's life treating you?" she asked. "Any girls on the horizon?"

"You ask me that all the time and the answer is always no."

"A girl can dream." Her fingers tightened around her cup of coffee. "Maybe I just want to live vicariously through you."

I snorted, closing my book. I wasn't going to be studying anytime soon. "The only one who will be living vicariously, sister, is me. One of these days, you're gonna find someone who sweeps you off your feet, and I won't be able to intimidate him."

Kaitlyn laughed. "Yeah, if this idiot ever gets his act together and actually asks me out."

"You know, you could be brave and ask him out if you really wanted to."

She shook her head. "Nah, his dad is one of my photography clients. I'm not going to be the one to cross that boundary. But if he asked me out... well, I'd probably say yes." She looked down at her drink, her cheeks turning slightly pink.

"Oh, I see, he's that cute."

"What? No. Shut up."

I poked her again. "Someone's got a crush."

"Shut up, dumbass. What are you studying?" she asked, pretending to look at my book, probably hoping I wouldn't notice her abrupt topic change.

I could let it slide this once. "Nothing interesting." It was the truth.

"Ready to be done? You've got what, two and a half months left?"

"Something like that."

"I noticed you haven't been working as hard lately," she said. "Why is that?"

"I might have come into some money," I admitted. "I don't have to take as many shifts now."

If I could tell anyone, it was Kaitlyn.

She leaned forward, resting her elbows on the table. "How did you come into money?" she asked. "And more importantly, why didn't I get any of it?"

"Can you keep a secret?" I asked, knowing full well that she could.

"Really?" She rolled her eyes. "You have to ask? Duh, of course I can."

"I may or may not have helped a very rich someone at the hotel with something, and they may or may not have given me several thousand dollars for helping them."

Kaitlyn's eyes widened. "Someone bribed you?" she hissed.

What? How could she even think that? "No, no, absolutely not." I shook my head. "No bribes involved. It was payment."

She narrowed her eyes suspiciously, taking a loud slurp of her coffee. "Are you gonna say anything else?" she finally asked. "I'm not sure I like the sound of this. It doesn't quite sound on the up and up. Why are you asking me to keep it a secret, anyway?"

"Well, this someone might have been someone related to the owner," I said slowly. "And she might not have had his permission to leave the hotel. And I might have helped her sneak out of the hotel and go out to see the sights for a little while."

Kaitlyn put down her cup. "You helped the owner's daughter sneak out?"

I picked up my own coffee and took a sip, not meeting Kaitlyn's eyes over the rim of the mug. "Maybe," I whispered into my drink.

"Keith, you could have gotten in so much trouble. Was it really worth it?"

I picked up my pen and started twirling it between my fingers. "Is twenty thousand dollars worth it?" I asked quietly.

Kaitlyn gasped, then clapped her hand over her mouth. "How much?" she whispered.

"Yeah," I said. "So, yeah, worth it."

"Hold on a second. You really got twenty thousand dollars to help an heiress sneak out of your hotel. And you didn't get caught by anyone?"

"Nope," I said, "nobody knows. Except you, now. You and Sarah."

Kaitlyn grinned. "So it's Sarah, is it? Not Miss Whatever-Her-Name-Is? You're on a first name basis with her."

That was my mistake. I knew better than to have called her that. Now Kaitlyn was going to be teasing me about it forever, especially if—or when—she found out that I would probably see Sarah again this weekend. That was if Kaitlyn didn't try to wrangle an invitation to meet her herself, probably to try to figure out how to get her own twenty thousand.

Actually, Kaitlyn wouldn't do that. I wouldn't put it past our youngest sister, Krystal, though.

"Look, you can't tell anyone," I said. "Promise?"

"Of course," she said, "I already promised. I'm not gonna break my promise just because I found out that you've been seeing an heiress."

"I'm not 'seeing her'," I protested.

"And yet you're on a first name basis with her."

I rolled my eyes and shrugged. "I'm just the bellhop to her. There's no way she even remembers my last name."

"She doesn't call you by your last name?" she asked.

"That would be a sign of respect, and if her father is any indication of the type of clients we have, none of them are showing us respect."

Especially not her father.

"Oh, rough, huh?"

I nodded. "Yeah, it's rough. He's not easy."

What else could I say, to my sister of all people? That Sarah's father was rude, that he didn't care about her or anyone else, that he'd barely even looked at me? That he never said thank you, and had no issues treating everyone, including his own daughter, like they didn't exist?

Kaitlyn had been out in the world for a little while, but we'd been sheltered from some harsh realities while growing up, and I wasn't going to be the one to tell her that those types of people existed. It was hard enough for me to understand, witnessing it. When you came from a family like ours, where the parents loved each other and the children were friends, where we didn't have that type of separation, I couldn't think of a way to even try to explain it.

How could I?

A family that didn't love each other was more foreign to us than just about anything. Because the Palmers may not have had much, but we had each other and we had love, and those were what mattered.

"Well, is she gonna come back?" Kaitlyn asked.

And here it was, the moment of truth. I wasn't going to lie to my sister.

I leaned in and whispered, "She might be coming back this weekend."

I was pretty sure most of the coffee shop heard Kaitlyn's not-so-quiet shriek.

And as much as I wanted to pretend that I wasn't excited too, if I had to admit it, I was excited to see Sarah again.

Sarah

It was probably the car sickness that made the ten-minute limo ride feel longer than the plane ride, even though it was a fraction of the time, right?

Flying in a private jet was easy. But that car ride at the end made the entire plane-ride full of anxiety, because I knew what was coming next.

Why did I have to be one of those people who got car sick? Why couldn't I be a normal person who could read in the car, for Pete's sake? A college friend had once told me that she'd read a book the entire time her family was road tripping during summer break, and I couldn't even look down at my phone without wanting to puke.

It wouldn't be so bad if Dad would talk to me, but my father was too interested in whatever phone call he was making to listen to me. Listening in on his phone call wasn't interesting enough to distract me from the nausea. Especially when I was pretty sure he used these car rides to practice being as vague as possible.

I chanced a quick glance at my phone. I'd texted Keith when we got off the plane, but so far, he hadn't answered me.

Maybe he was working.

Or maybe he decided that I wasn't worth the trouble I could cause him, and he was just going to ignore me.

Hopefully that wasn't it.

My brain was very fond of worst case scenarios, and this was a particularly easy one.

That's all this was, just my anxiety acting up again. It was fine. Keith wasn't ignoring me because I was annoying him, or because he'd gotten tired of me, or because he didn't want to see me again.

It was just my brain being stupid.

Again.

Right?

I'd thought about texting Keith a lot in the month since we'd met, but what did you say to a guy who had saved your life because he was afraid of losing his job?

Not that he'd only saved my life because of his job, but you know.

It had just been so much fun getting a glimpse of normal with him, and I was hoping desperately that he would want to do it again.

I was really scared that he wouldn't.

Because if he wouldn't, I was going to be very bored this weekend.

When my phone buzzed, I glanced down at it really quickly.

Nope. Still no text. Just a stupid email.

Dad hung up his current phone call and I opened my mouth to ask what his plans were this weekend when his phone rang again.

Typical.

"Hello," he said. "What do you need?" Of course, he was willing to ask that of anyone but his daughter.

My phone buzzed again. Just Mom, responding to my text saying that we'd arrived safely. Her answer simply said that she was glad we'd made it, and she loved me.

Mom never came on these business trips. She, like me, had been raised to be a proper society wife, staying home, attending functions, overseeing the raising the children, doing charity work, all those good and lovely things that I would be doing for the rest of my life, whether I wanted to or not.

Right now, it was "or not."

But I was here because this was who I was raised to be, and unless I managed to find someone who fit Dad's standards and also didn't care about me being the perfect society wife, it would be what I did until the day I died.

Or the day my husband died. If that one came first, I'd be free to do whatever I wanted.

I wished Mom would come on these trips, though. Then at least I would have someone to talk to. But she and Dad had no interest in spending more time with each other than was necessary, and I couldn't blame her. I knew all too well what it was like being with Dad for a long stretch of time. How she had put up with it for so many years, I didn't know.

Her hefty allowance probably had something to do with it.

It didn't matter though. She had her role and I had mine. And as soon as I'd gone off to school, our paths hadn't crossed much.

She'd been there to help me set up my first bank account that Dad didn't know about, though.

And she'd been there to counsel me on how to manage the society boys who would try to win me over.

She'd been there for those moments, but not for the rest.

She hadn't been there for my first period. My first crush. My first heartbreak.

But that was how our life was. She and I were trophy wives—or a future trophy wife, in my case—there to look good on the arm of a man who was too busy to spend time with those who he loved, or who he was supposed to love.

There to give him children, take care of his philanthropic work, and make him look good, especially if he was too much of a jerk to do it himself.

So she kept busy with her charity work, which gave her a purpose now that I was grown and kept her conveniently too busy to go with Dad on his work trips.

And I was paraded around the country, waiting to find someone I could stand to spend the rest of my life with.

Dad's phone call ended and he looked up at me for the first time since we'd boarded the plane. "Sarah, I do believe we'll have brunch again tomorrow. Julian is excited to see you."

"Of course," I said, though I was the opposite of excited to see Julian again. Our last visit had proved that he was exactly like all of the others who came before him. Selfish, a little bit of a jerk, cared only about himself, and spent more time looking at my boobs than he did paying attention to what I said.

They were all raised the same way, so why did I keep expecting to find one who would be different? Why did I dare to dream that there was someone out there for me who was kind, and sweet, and wanted to know my opinion, and cared about me when I was upset, and kept me from almost dying, and defended me... and most definitely was not Keith Palmer.

I sighed as I realized that once again, my thoughts were trending in a dangerous direction.

Keith was not for me. He never could be. And I had to stop thinking about him like that.

But that was difficult to do when my heart skipped a beat every time my phone buzzed, though it was never him responding. After the first night, when he'd responded he was glad I'd made it back safely, I hadn't heard from him again until a single "okay" last night.

Maybe he didn't like texting?

This was foolishness. Pure, utter foolishness.

I could see the hotel in the distance and my heart started to beat a little faster. Would Keith be there this evening? It wasn't entirely out of the realm of possibility. I'd hoped that he would be able to start working less after he earned twenty thousand in one night. But the fact that he hadn't texted more hopefully meant that he was there and not just ignoring me. I didn't think the bellhops were allowed to have their phones on them. So, there was a chance. It wasn't like I'd done anything worth being ignored for, either.

As the limo pulled into the drive, my stomach tensed, and not just from the car ride. There was a quiet moment as I waited for the limo door to open, gathering my purse and putting my sunglasses on, and then it opened and there was Keith, holding his hand out for me.

I couldn't hide my smile as I swung my legs out of the limo and took his hand, allowing him to help me to my feet.

"Good evening, Miss Hanson," he said, his voice deeper than I remembered. "I hope you had a pleasant drive." He winked at me before letting go of my hand and butterflies erupted in my stomach, replacing the nausea completely.

"It's good to be back," I said, hoping that he would know what I meant and my father would have no clue. Not that he was paying any attention as he walked towards the door of the hotel without even looking to see if I would follow.

"I'll get your bags," Keith said, following my gaze to my father.

I followed Dad into the hotel, noting that it was the same manager behind the front desk. As Dad grabbed the room keys from the manager, I walked towards the elevator, Keith following close behind me. "It's good to see you again," I said in what I hoped was a normal enough tone that Dad wouldn't notice. It wasn't anything more than pleasant small talk, anyway.

"It's a pleasure to see you too, Miss Hanson," Keith said as the elevator doors opened and the three of us walked in. Dad didn't bother to press the elevator button—such a task was beneath him—so Keith leaned over to press it.

The ride to the penthouse seemed to take forever with Dad staring at his phone, making somewhat angry sounds more than once. I could see Keith trying not to look at him, clearly wondering what he was doing, while either far too polite or too scared of losing his job to say anything about how weirdly uncomfortable it was.

When Dad opened the penthouse doors, he quickly walked into his bedroom and slammed the door behind him, leaving Keith and me in the common area, staring at each other.

"I thought you didn't have to work anymore," I said, setting my purse down on the side table. "What happened to that?"

"I haven't been working nearly as much," he said as he picked up the smaller of the two bags. "Is this one yours?"

"It is," I said, and he walked it over to my room. "If you're not working as much, why are you here?"

Okay, Sarah, no need to be so desperate. You wanted him to be here and now you're asking why he is?

Clearly, I'm not good at dealing with guys who don't want anything from me.

"Well, I heard that we might need a little extra help this evening," he said with a smile, "so I thought I'd take a shift." Then, with a glance at my father's closed door, his voice dropped to a whisper. "Besides, I didn't want you to have to bribe another poor bellhop. The rest of them might not take it so well. And who knows? Then you might start to get a reputation of giving up a little extra something for helpful people and then you'd be stuck bribing everyone for everything, and that's no good."

The tension in my hands relaxed and I grinned. "Does that mean I have to bribe you?"

He closed my bedroom door behind him and walked over to me, stepping just into my personal space. "No bribes required," he said softly. "But you might find a present with your bag."

I glanced over at my closed door. "How—"

He took a step back and winked. "Can I get you anything else this evening, Miss Hanson? I'm working tonight until eleven, and tomorrow until three, so if there's anything I can do for you while I'm here, please let me know."

"What are you doing tomorrow night?" I asked quietly, a grin appearing on my face despite me trying to stop it.

He cocked his head and shrugged. "I'm hanging out with a friend, but I don't know what we're doing. I think I'll let my friend decide."

Hanging out with Keith and getting to make the decision about what we were doing? It sounded like a fantastic evening to me.

Waiting shouldn't have been this hard. And yet here I was, as anxious as could be, waiting for the elevator doors to open and Sarah to walk through. My foot anxiously tapped against the luxurious rug that muffled the sound of my nervous action.

I'd told the others that I had a friend coming in this weekend and she was staying here, but that she and I would be heading out for the evening. It had seemed enough to distract them from the fact that I was sitting in the lobby waiting.

But they had their eyes peeled for an heiress, so hopefully, Sarah would look nothing like one.

When the elevator doors opened and she walked through wearing my hoodie and baseball cap, my stomach lurched. It was the moment of truth.

Would they recognize her? Or would the disguise be enough?

I stood, meeting her halfway with a hug. "I told them you were a friend," I whispered as she stepped into my arms with a look of confusion. "It needs to look believable."

She accepted the reason without complaint and returned the hug, settling into my arms like she belonged there.

This was dangerous.

I quickly let go, looking over my shoulder at the bellhops and the front desk. None of them were paying attention to us. I put myself between them and her and shepherded her through the front doors.

"Well, that was easy," she said when we were a safe distance away.

"As long as they didn't recognize you," I said.

"Do you think they did?" Her voice went higher and she looked back at the hotel.

"No, no, no, don't look," I said. That would only give them another chance to see her if they were suspicious. "You're fine. They weren't expecting me to be meeting you."

"They wouldn't expect Sarah Hanson to look like this even if they thought it was me," she said, gesturing to my college sweatshirt. I had to admit, it looked good on her. "Thank you for letting me borrow this. It's very comfortable."

"It's warm too, which doesn't hurt."

"No, it doesn't," she said, snuggling into it. "It's pretty chilly out."

It had definitely gotten colder in the past month, though I was still comfortable in my jeans and long-sleeved shirt. But since she was from Southern California, she probably wasn't used to the cold the way we were. "I thought it might help," I said. "I doubt you have any hoodies with you, or if you do, they probably wouldn't blend in as well."

She grinned, taking her hands out of the hoodie pocket to swing them as we walked down the sidewalk. "Yeah, most of my layers are not hoodies like this. They're cardigans or blazers. I think my dad would die if he knew I was walking down the street in a hoodie."

I tried not to focus on how cute she looked in my sweatshirt. I tried to ignore the way it made me feel, but that was hard to do as she looked at me, laughing, settling my baseball cap more firmly on her head.

I was playing with fire and I was going to get burned.

"You know, I've been thinking about this for a month now," she said. "I really, really wanted to be here again. With you. Not in the hotel room. So, you know, I'm really glad I was able to get out. Thank you for taking me."

"Well, I've been thinking about it too," I admitted. "I had a lot of fun last time—I hope you did too."

I'd probably had a little too much fun with her last time.

And I was setting myself up for trouble again.

"Are we going to go to the same place?" she asked. "I liked the music there."

"And the dancing?" I asked.

Her cheeks turned a pale shade of pink. "I may or may not have practiced in the past month."

I looked down at her, not sure what to make of that. "You've been practicing line dancing."

"Yes."

"You, the California heiress, have been practicing line dancing."

Her cheeks turned even darker. "Yes, I've been practicing in my room, where Dad can't see me. A pair of earbuds and he's none the wiser."

I grinned. "We can go to the same place if that's what you want. I don't have a problem with that. I'll have to see how much you've improved, because I haven't improved at all."

"What, you mean you didn't have lots of free time to practice line dancing?" she asked, tilting her head.

"Imagine that, I was too busy."

The smile on her face was infectious. "I guess I'll just have to be better than you."

"I bet you're better than me at a lot of things, not just line dancing."

"Probably. But I'm sure you have your own strengths."

I snorted as we paused at a stoplight, waiting to cross. "Yeah, apparently, sneaking women out of my workplace."

She was silent for a minute. "Have you, well—"

"Have I snuck someone else out?"

She nodded. "Yeah."

"I'll have you know, this is only the second time I've ever done it, and I have a one hundred percent success rate."

She smirked as the light changed and looked both ways before stepping into the street. "Yeah, I totally believe that."

"Hey now, don't go giving me a bad reputation. I should have the opposite of a bad reputation."

"You mean a good reputation."

"Well yes, when you say it like that it sounds better."

"Maybe I'm just helping you find the right words," she said.

"And what words are those?"

"The right ones," she said, her eyes dancing.

"Oh, stop," I said, gently shoving her with my elbow. "You're just trying to get me flustered, like I'm the twelve-year-old boy meeting the gorgeous babysitter for the first time. Not that I have previous experience with that or anything. Totally vague. Not at all a memorable incident. I'm just gonna stop talking now. You can talk the rest of the way there."

Shut the hell up, Keith. You're embarrassing yourself.

"Maybe I like hearing you talk."

I looked down at her and she grinned, elbowing me back. "You know exactly what you're doing," I said.

She was having the time of her life, was what she was doing.

And it was freaking adorable to watch.

"So, what do you normally do?" I asked. "Practice line dancing all day?"

She shrugged as we waited for the next crosswalk. "Not much right now, since I've graduated. I'm pretty much just preparing to get married to a rich man so I can be the perfect society wife, raise my children, and make him look good."

I whipped my head around to stare at her, trying to decide if she was joking, but there wasn't any hint of sarcasm, just raw honesty that hinted at the hurt underneath it.

"That's it?"

"Yeah, that's why I go on these trips. My dad is taking me around to introduce me to his friends and their sons, the eligible bachelors. All of them boring as hell and more interested in the way I look than anything." Her voice wobbled.

So she was being reduced to her ability to be a trophy wife, rather than her ability to be herself? She was being forced into a box that she didn't belong in.

"And you don't get any say in it?" I asked.

"Well, so far I've managed to avoid marrying the worst of them. Julian here, he's...interesting. This is the second time we'll be meeting him, so we'll see how long I can avoid anything more than superficial brunches."

"Interesting in a good way?"

She chewed on her lip and didn't answer.

"Did you meet him here last time?" I asked, slightly changing the topic since she didn't want to answer that question.

"I did. We had brunch and he spent most of it staring at, well, not my face, and I spent most of it wishing that he would actually ask me a decent question." She sighed, her mouth pressing into a line. "But it doesn't matter. I don't really want to talk about it. I want to enjoy tonight, without thinking about what my life is meant to be, and just have a fun evening with a friend."

"Oh, we're friends now," I said, attempting to bring some light-heartedness back after I'd taken it too far.

"Of course we're friends," she said, her voice and words displaying more confidence than her face. Was she concerned that she'd offended me? "Didn't you say we were friends in the lobby?"

"I feel special now."

She looked up at me with a smile. "You should."

She didn't say anything else. Was she overthinking the way I was?

When the light changed, I looked both ways before resting my hand on the small of her back and ushering her across the street. She stiffened at my touch, but before we reached the sidewalk, she'd relaxed and moved closer to me, her arm brushing against my torso.

Did she realize she'd done that?

I found myself reluctant to remove my hand, but the bar was on the corner and there were only a few steps left. When I stepped away to open the door, she leaned like she was going to come with me, and I had to stop myself from reaching out to touch her again as we entered McGuire's.

I looked down at her, putting a professional distance between us, and smiled at her grin.

She looked up at me, bouncing on her toes slightly as a loud country song played. "Do you want to drink first, or do you want to go dance?" I asked.

She looked between the bar and the dance floor, her indecision filling the air.

"Why don't I go get you a drink while you dance one dance," I said, "and then we can get a little buzz before you drag me out there."

"Okay," she said quickly, her smile spreading from ear to ear. She pushed her way through the crowd towards the dance floor and I watched as she took her place in the line and executed the steps perfectly.

She really did have a lot of time to practice, huh?

She was nothing like the fumbling girl of last time, who'd been just as bad as me at line dancing. She looked like she belonged out there—all she needed was a cowboy hat and some boots.

If she came back again, I could get her some. She'd probably light up like the sun. I'd have to ask her shoe size though, so it wouldn't be a surprise. Unless I took her bowling and found out that way.

I rolled my eyes at myself and walked over to the bar.

She was not my girlfriend.

We were not dating.

I should not be planning future excursions and surprises like we were.

She was my boss's daughter, and I was taking care of her so that nothing bad would happen. This was strictly good business. Nothing more.

I got to the bar and asked for a beer and a margarita and an order of mozzarella sticks, and soon enough, the song was over and she was meeting me at the small table that I'd found.

"I knew that one," she said, her eyes glowing. "So much fun.'"

"You looked like you were having a blast." I handed her the margarita.

"Thank you." She took a sip. "Oh, I forgot, I'm going to need some food."

At that exact moment, a waitress appeared with the plate of mozzarella sticks. "Here you go."

"You remembered," Sarah said, her eyes lighting up. "Thank you," she told the waitress.

"Of course I remembered. And I don't want to see you forget your two drink rule—although I kinda sorta do."

She laughed and dunked a mozzarella stick in marinara sauce. "Yeah, I bet you want to see that."

"Do you blame me?" I asked.

"Oh, I don't blame you," she said with her mouth full. "Very predictable though–you should work on that."

"You want me to be less predictable?" I asked.

"Exactly. Predictable isn't fun. I deal with predictable all day. A little less predictable would be more exciting."

"You want exciting?"

"At this point, I would do just about anything for something other than predictable, whether it was exciting or not. I don't want my predictable anymore." She stared off at the dance floor, suddenly pensive.

"But you don't have a choice, do you?" I asked. This was veering off into dangerous territory again, but I had to know.

"Not unless I want to be disowned," she said. "And I suppose I would survive, but I don't know that I'm prepared for that. I have no skills. I have a degree, but no actual knowledge of how to do anything with it. My mom helped me start an 'oh shit' fund, but in this world, with no practical skills, that would only go so far."

"But you don't want the life that your father has planned for you, do you?" Not that it was any of my business, but I was curious. And the way she hadn't stopped talking yet made me wonder if she'd been waiting for someone to ask about this.

Sarah sighed, reaching for another mozzarella stick. "No, I don't want the life that my father has planned for me. But I don't have a choice right now."

"If you could," I asked, "what would you choose?"

She looked at me with a sad smile. "If I could?" she asked. "I don't even know what. I don't know, a man who loved me for me, children who he wanted for more than having an heir. Something that fulfilled me, not just a marriage where I'm a trophy wife to one of these dumbasses my father keeps trying to set me up with. None of them care about me or my boundaries, and it sucks. You know, one of them even tried to kiss me, even though I already told him I didn't want to kiss anyone until marriage."

Wait, what?

That was new information.

"You don't want to kiss anyone until you're married?" I asked, trying to keep my tone neutral, even though that was the last thing I wanted to do. Did she think this was something normal? Was this what heiresses were raised to believe in? "Is there a particular reason?"

Sarah shrugged, looking over at the dance floor. "My whole life has been arranged for me. This is one of the few things that I can control. And in doing so, I can do my best to make sure that the man I do choose to marry will respect my choices, whether he agrees with them or not. Because I highly doubt there are many men out there who are willing to wait until marriage to kiss me. It's a small bit of control that has helped me so far turn down just about every man my father has pushed me at, and it's something he's highly frustrated with. But since personal principles are one of the things he's tried to hammer into my head my whole life, he can't say anything about it."

I blinked at her a couple of times, trying to organize my thoughts.

It was actually solid logic, even if every part of me wanted to take offense at the thought of not kissing until marriage.

How did she expect any guy to wait that long to kiss her, much less someone who actually loved her?

"So that's your loophole," I said after a moment.

She grinned, taking a sip of her margarita. "I guess that's my loophole."

My mind was seriously blown at the idea of this no kissing thing.

"So really, no kissing at all? Like, you've never kissed anyone?"

"Never kissed anyone," she confirmed. "Honestly, it's been pretty easy so far. There hasn't really been anyone I've wanted to break my own rules with. Certainly none of the guys my dad has tried to set me up with, and I don't meet many other guys."

"Well, it's a good thing I would never kiss the boss's daughter," I joked, "so it won't be an issue with me."

But even as I joked, suddenly part of me could picture kissing her with full clarity.

Well fudge me running.

Judging by the pink tone in her cheeks, maybe she was thinking about it, too.

Oops. I probably shouldn't have said that.

"Are you ready to dance?" I asked in an attempt to change the subject, then drained the last of my beer, ready to distract myself from the sudden images of us bombarding my brain.

"Oh, yes, let's," she said before chugging the rest of her margarita and standing, reaching out for my hand, and dragging me onto the dance floor, her hand fitting so perfectly into mine.

But being out on the dance floor wasn't the distraction I'd hoped for. Even though it was a country line dance, we still kept brushing into each other, and every time we touched, electric sparks ran through me. Where before there had been a subtle appreciation of how beautiful she was, now it was all I could think about. Every time I looked down at her, I saw her beautiful brown eyes sparkling with pride as she executed the dance perfectly. Every time I heard her laugh when I messed up and bumped into her, it made me want to bump into her on purpose. Every time she twirled past me, I caught a whiff of her perfume, which managed to be delicately floral without smelling like an old lady.

The music was loud, but not loud enough to distract me from the thoughts that suddenly plagued me.

Why did I have to make that stupid joke?

We stayed for another hour, dancing for most of it, but when she looked at her watch, then up at me with regret in her eyes, I knew it was time to wrap things up and head back before she got in trouble.

Even though I didn't want the night to end.

As we walked back, I let my hand rest on her lower back again, guiding her across the crosswalk. But this time, I didn't have to let go until we were within sight of the hotel.

"Thank you," she said, looking up at me and taking a step back, putting distance between us. "I had a wonderful evening."

"I did too." The words didn't seem adequate, but I couldn't think of what else to say, suddenly tongue-tied.

"Are you sure I can't pay you for helping me?" she asked.

"Absolutely sure. I don't need it—this was fun enough."

"What if you get in trouble?" she asked. "What if somebody finds out?"

"It would be worth it." I reached over and pulled the baseball cap further down on her face, hiding those gorgeous eyes. "Let me know when you're back safely, please. Do you want me to go in with you?"

"Probably best if you don't," she said. "I'll be less noticeable without you."

I knew she was right, but everything in me was screaming to walk with her as she took a step away from me. "Have a good night, Sarah," I said before she got too far.

She turned halfway, smiling over her shoulder. "You too, Keith."

I watched as she walked into the hotel, waiting for her to disappear behind the doors before I started walking to my car.

It had been a fun evening, if a little surprising.

She really didn't want to kiss anyone until marriage?

I couldn't imagine any of the self-entitled boys who I'd met at the hotel would put up with that.

Heck, would I put up with that?

Obviously, I would, because I was a Palmer and my mother would literally kill me if I didn't respect my girlfriend and every other woman.

But if it wasn't about basic human decency, would I be okay with my girlfriend not wanting to kiss until marriage?

Well, I guess for the right girl, I would put up with anything.

Unfortunately, Sarah was not the right girl for me.

I wouldn't have to worry about it, because she wasn't mine and never would be.

November

Saturday, November 5th

KP: *Well, was this one a winner?*
12:36 pm

*Haha. Very funny. He was even worse than the last one.
I swear he was trying to smell my hair.*
12:45 pm

KP: *Ew. Where does your dad find them? Hasn't he run out of colleagues by now?*
12:57 pm

I'm starting to think they're just random guys he meets on the golf course. Like "oh, you're single? Bring your dad for lunch on me, I'll introduce you to my highly eligible daughter."

1:12 pm

KP: *Is it at least a good lunch?*

1:14 pm

LOL no. It's not.

1:15 pm

Saturday, November 12th

Surprise, we're coming today! Early this afternoon. I didn't know until just now. Are you working?

9:22 am

KP: *Nope. Tonight?*
9:34 am

I might see if Dad will let me meet up with a "college friend." How high does your voice go?
9:36 am

KP: *It doesn't.*
9:37 am

Sarah

When Dad sprung a surprise trip on me, the only thing I could think of was if Keith would be busy or not. Since the night at the bar, we'd started texting. And as much as I knew we shouldn't be doing this, I couldn't stop myself.

There was no harm in texting a friend, right?

So I'd kept talking to him, and I'd enjoyed every minute of it.

But since he'd said that he wouldn't be working today, I was going to see if Dad would let me leave the hotel for an afternoon. I waited until we were in the limo, almost to the hotel, before trying to get Dad's attention.

"What?" he asked, looking up from his phone for half a second.

"A friend of mine from college just moved here and was asking if I would be able to spend the day with them."

He looked up from his phone again. "What are you going to do?" Dad asked.

"There was something said about a museum? I thought it would be fun to spend the afternoon away from the hotel. I'd be back in time for an early evening, of course. And I'm sure we have a brunch or lunch tomorrow."

"Yes, brunch," Dad confirmed. "I guess you can go, as long as you're back by eight."

"Thank you," I said. I stayed as calm as I could outwardly, but I was jumping for joy inside.

He actually said I could go.

"Who are you going with?" Dad asked.

"I was talking to my college friend Susan," I said smoothly, having prepared for this already.

There was no need to tell him that Susan actually lived in Alaska and would not be anywhere near here. But I had sent her a happy birthday text earlier, so that counted as talking to her. It wasn't a lie.

Dad grunted and went back to his phone.

I was buzzing with excitement the rest of the ride there.

I was actually going on a Dad-sanctioned day trip.

The details might have been stretching the truth, but the part where I was going out with a friend wasn't.

And he had no idea.

I felt a little bad about lying to him, but only so much.

If he didn't want me to lie to him, he shouldn't give me such meaningless restrictions. A girl ought to be able to go out and see a friend when she's in town, not spend the entire time cooped up in a hotel room, right?

When we got to the hotel, a different bellhop helped me out of the car and took our luggage up to the penthouse. I smiled and said thank you, wondering if he and Keith were friends.

Had Keith told them that he'd met me?

Twenty minutes later, I was anxiously waiting in my room for a text from Keith. He was supposed to tell me when he was close to the hotel, so that I could leave hopefully without Dad seeing him. Although if Dad did, for some reason, come down to the lobby, I could just tell him that Keith was a rideshare driver.

But Dad probably wouldn't notice. He probably wouldn't even notice me leaving.

I had butterflies and they would not go away.

I didn't want to have butterflies. I knew that Keith wasn't part of my future, but the idea of a day with him had me thrilled to my core.

Was he excited to see me too? Did he also have butterflies?

The butterflies were getting so violent that they'd almost become nausea by the time I got a text that said, *I'll be there in five minutes.*

I grabbed my purse, opened my door and saw that Dad wasn't in the common room, and walked out of the suite.

He never said anything to me when he left, so why should I bother saying anything to him? Especially when drawing his attention could potentially make him change his mind?

No, there was no reason to say anything.

I took the elevator and walked through the lobby, half-expecting someone to stop me or for my dad to call and demand to know where I was.

When I made it down the block to where Keith was waiting at the corner, everything in me felt free and clear. As I opened the door of his little SUV, Keith looked over at me and grinned. "You made it out? I'm shocked."

"I know, right?" I slid into the seat, and I wanted to reach over and give him a hug. But that felt too forward. And a handshake wouldn't work.

High five?

I don't know. It was weird.

What did you do when someone picked you up, someone who was not your boyfriend, someone who was maybe only your friend because it was his job?

It was too complicated, so I didn't do anything, just sat there somewhat uncomfortably until Keith turned on the country music station and one of the songs that played at the bar came on.

I'd been listening to this song on repeat for a month, and I couldn't resist singing along.

"You like this one?" Keith asked.

You can't interrupt singing to respond to someone. It just isn't done. So when there was an appropriate break in the song, I said, "it's one of my favorites," before continuing to sing.

Keith was polite enough to wait until the song ended before asking, "What did you want to do with your free day? I've just been driving home on autopilot. We could go see that museum, or we could keep heading to my hometown, or whatever else you want."

"What is there to do?" I twirled my fingers through the end of my ponytail. "I don't even know where you live."

"I live in this little town called Hosta Falls," he said. "It's full of some of the best people you'll ever meet—and some of the strangest people you'll ever meet—but it's home. They mean well, but sometimes it can be a bit much."

"What do you mean?" I asked. "Is it really that weird?"

"I mean, it's probably not, but you have no experience with small towns, do you?"

"No, no small town experience here. I live in one of the biggest cities in the country."

"Well, small towns have their own special breed of people. My parents are very well known, since my mom owns her own shop on the square, and–."

"Your mom owns her own shop?" I interrupted.

Keith smiled. "She does. It's called Chickadee Lane and it's a place for women, especially young mothers, to come together to take classes and meet with each other. And she sells some merchandise that she's designed. It's really a cool thing."

The pride was so evident in his voice, it made me homesick, though for what, I wasn't even sure. Could you be homesick for someone or something that you'd never even met or experienced? Maybe it wasn't really homesickness, but it felt like it, that yearning to be somewhere different.

I didn't feel it very often for my own home. Home was a multi-millionaire's mansion, cold and bleak and empty. Mom tried to warm it up a little, but she could only do so much. But the comfort and happiness in Keith's voice when he talked about his mother's store gave me a lump in my throat.

"We could go visit your mother's shop," I said.

"We could, but that's not gonna take all day. Unfortunately, there's not too much to do or see in Hosta Falls."

"Where does the name come from?" I asked. "Is there a waterfall?"

He grinned. "Actually, yes. Do you like hiking?"

I thought about it for a second. The closest thing I'd ever done to hiking was maybe going for a walk in a park? "I probably haven't been hiking the way you would describe it, but I would be open to trying it."

He looked off into the distance to think about it. "The trail to the waterfall isn't that bad, so you could probably do it." He looked down at my feet. "Although we may need to stop by our house and borrow my mom's or one of my sister's' hiking boots. What size shoe do you wear?"

"Sevens."

"Oh perfect, you'll fit in at least half of their shoes, I think. We can swing by home and grab those if you want to see the waterfall."

I wasn't really the adventurous type, but after seeing how happy he was about it, trekking through the woods with Keith was the only thing I wanted to do with my day. "I like that idea," I said. "Maybe I'll get to meet some of your family, too."

But when we got to the Palmer home, nobody was there. If I had to guess, they were probably all at work or school. "I'm sorry, I know you wanted to meet them. Maybe if we bring the boots back before we have to go? But come on, let's go see if Mom's boots will fit you." Keith led the way down a hallway and disappeared into a bedroom.

I paused outside the door, not sure if I should follow him into his parents' bedroom.

But Keith called out for me, "Come on, what are you waiting for?"

So I entered the room and found myself in the coziest bedroom I'd ever been in. Completely opposite from the sterile hotel rooms and cold and forbidding rooms of my father's house, it was full of warmth and love. Was this how normal people decorated their homes?

There wasn't even that much there. It was a clean, well-lit room with a cream bedspread, bright curtains, and light wooden furniture. A couple of plants added color and warmth to the room.

I wanted a room like this when I moved out. When I had my own home.

"What a beautiful room," I said to no one in particular. "I like the way it's furnished."

"You could furnish your own bedroom like this," Keith said from the depths of the closet.

"No, my dad probably wouldn't like it."

He poked his head out and stared at me. "Your dad decides how you decorate your bedroom?"

I looked around the room, so different from everything I know. "Yeah."

Keith looked vaguely disapproving. "You deserve more than that," he said, before disappearing back into the closet.

I knew that I deserved more than that. I'd known that for most of my life. But for the first time in a very long time, or maybe ever, I was starting to actually believe that I did deserve more than that.

But I wasn't sure I would be able to change it.

Honestly, he probably wouldn't even notice if I changed my bedroom, but he certainly wouldn't approve if he found out about it. It wouldn't match the modern aesthetic of the rest of the house.

"Here they are," Keith said, emerging from the closet with a pair of hiking boots in his hand. "Hopefully they fit, but if not, we'll raid my sister Kaitlyn's closet next."

"You're sure they won't mind?" I asked, reaching out to take the hiking boots from him.

"I promise."

So, I sat down on the edge of the bed and took my shoes off, slipping my feet into Mrs. Palmer's hiking boots. They were a tiny bit big, but honestly, for being someone else's shoes, they fit pretty well.

"I think they'll work," I said.

Keith knelt in front of me and my heart leaped into my throat at the sight of him on one knee. Completely oblivious to my internal panic, he felt around the toe of the boot. "Oh yeah, that'll work, especially since it's not a massive trail. You probably won't even need them, but better safe than sorry. I don't know what you told your dad, but I probably shouldn't bring you back with your shoes covered in mud or with a broken ankle."

"You can get a broken ankle from hiking?" I asked.

"Nah, not on this trail with hiking boots," he said.

"You're sure?" I asked.

"It's a super flat trail and half of it is a boardwalk. I won't let you break your ankle." He grinned. "Come on, let's go."

We jumped back into his car and drove for maybe fifteen minutes before passing the sign for the Hosta Falls State Park. "Here we are," Keith said as we pulled into the parking lot. "There are' only a couple trails here, but the waterfall one is my favorite."

"I'm excited." I followed him out of the car, watching as he grabbed a backpack from the backseat and tossed his keys into it. "What's in that?"

"It's got some water and snacks and a small first aid kit."

"Do you go hiking often, then?" I asked, following him towards the trailhead.

"No, I don't go hiking often. It's my car emergency kit, but it also works well for hiking, or really anything, since I keep it in a bag. It's just nice to be able to take it with me."

The trailhead wasn't far from the parking lot, and as we entered the woods, I took a deep breath, feeling a peace run through me that I hadn't felt in a very long time.

"This is beautiful," I said, looking around at the trees.

"You haven't even seen the best part yet."

"Did you go hiking more often growing up?" I asked.

"Not as often as my mom would have liked, but more than my sisters wanted to." Keith grinned.

"Your sisters are not big outdoors people then?"

"No, not particularly." He held a large branch aside for me. "Kaitlyn is probably the most outdoorsy, followed by Krystal, and Kathryn just loves her books."

"So, Kathryn is the book sibling," I said, more to myself than to him.

"What?"

"Oh, just trying to get your siblings straight in my head. There are so many of them, it's hard to keep track."

"Well, yes, Kathryn is the book sibling. She would spend all day, every day at the library if we let her."

"What's stopping her now?"

"Oh, nothing. School, I guess. If she wasn't in school, she'd probably be working at the library. She volunteered there for years."

"And Krystal?" I asked. "What's her story?"

"Krystal is a spitfire who loves driving everyone crazy, and despite that, she loves everyone with her whole heart. That's why we put up with her." He grinned. "And then Kaitlyn is probably my favorite. Don't tell anybody."

"Who am I going to tell?" I asked.

"I don't know," he said with a shrug. "You might tell some other bellhops who you make friends with."

"You're the only bellhop I talk to." I looked away from him, at the scenery on either side of us. "You're the only one who even looks at me."

"Really?"

"I think everyone else is too scared of my dad."

"He is rather intimidating."

I laughed, sarcasm dripping from my voice as I said, "He's not that intimidating, Keith."

He was extremely intimidating, even for me, his daughter. Maybe especially me. The only ones who didn't seem to be intimidated by him were his college buddies and their sons, which led me to believe they were all cut from the same cloth.

"Honestly, I think your dad is a whole lot of bravado, and if we really broke it down and figured him out, he wouldn't be nearly as scary as a lot of people think he is."

"You may be right about that, but I'm not sure I want to test that theory."

Keith laughed. "I'm not sure I want to test that theory either. I can talk a good game, but he is still your father."

"Does that mean you're scared of him? Because he's my father? Or because he's him?" I asked, suddenly curious to find out the answer and a little unsure if I wanted the honest truth.

"Because he's your father," Keith said. "You can't spend time with a beautiful woman without being a little scared of her father."

Suddenly, I couldn't even look at him. "You think I'm beautiful?" I asked softly.

"Sarah, you are gorgeous," he said. He stopped walking and turned to look at me, waiting until I made eye contact to keep talking, like he was trying to make sure that his words had the full effect. "I didn't tell you before because you know, you're the boss's daughter and I didn't want to be weird. But you are beautiful. And I really appreciate your friendship."

"Friendship, hmm? So we're friends?" I teased.

Keith started walking again, shaking his head at me. "Haven't you already asked me that?"

I grinned at him.

"Yes, we're friends," he said. "Not sure why I would put up with risking my life otherwise."

"You think you're risking your life every time you see me? Very funny."

"Well, I do think that your father might have me killed if he found out I was sneaking you out, so yeah, I think I might be risking my life."

I couldn't help myself, I laughed. "You're ridiculous."

"You're ridiculous-er."

"That's not a real word."

"It's a real word to me," he said, sticking his tongue out.

"So mature."

He grinned. "I know, it's my best quality."

Before I could answer, I heard the sound of water rushing by. He must have been able to tell, because he grinned at me again.

"Yes, that's it," he said in response to my questioning look. "We're almost there."

"Almost there" was right. Barely a minute later, we turned a corner in the trail, and there it was.

Hosta Falls.

"Beautiful," I said.

"I think so, but I wouldn't have snuck you out here if I didn't think so."

"I suppose that's true."

I stood there, taking in the sights of the waterfall. It wasn't very tall, nor was it a huge amount of water. But since most of my experience with water features was in public parks and fountains, to see such a pretty waterfall in nature was truly one of the most beautiful sights I'd ever seen.

"You should see it when the hostas are blooming," Keith said, sitting down on a large rock. "It's one of my favorite things in the world."

"I'll just have to come back for that," I said, sitting next to him.

"That sounds like a plan," he said softly, and I realized just how close we were.

But I didn't mind.

The sound of the water rushing and birds chirping and a soft breeze filled the air as the distance between us felt smaller and smaller.

Keith cleared his throat and looked away, breaking the spell.

"Are you hungry, my lady?" he asked, reaching for his bag.

I didn't realize I was until he said it, but now eating was the only thing I could think about.

"Yes, actually," I admitted.

"Then it's a good thing I happened to bring snacks." Keith opened his bag and pulled out two bottles of water and a variety of granola bars. "Ladies first," he said, holding the stack out to me.

I chose one of my favorites and he grabbed one for himself before putting the rest back in the bag. We ate in silence, sitting on a rock near the edge of the river to watch the waterfall.

"Have you ever fallen off of these rocks?" I asked as I crumpled the wrapper into a ball and shoved it into my pocket.

"You probably don't want to know the answer to that," he said with a grin.

"So that's a yes."

He shrugged. "What you and my mother don't know won't hurt you."

"So you're saying I should be careful when I stand up?" I asked, looking around for something to hold on to.

"I'll help you, don't worry." He got to his feet, reaching out for me. As I took his hand and started to stand, one of my feet went out from under me and I started slipping down towards the waterfall. My heart leaped into my throat as I fell into open space, sliding down a damp, mossy rock, before my arm pulled tight in his grasp and he was reaching down to grab my other arm, pulling me back to safety.

Keith pulled me close, his arm wrapped securely around my waist. "You jinxed it," he said, holding me as I started to tremble from the adrenaline.

"I didn't mean to jinx it," I protested. Once again, Keith Palmer had saved my life. "What is it with me almost getting hurt every time we're together?"

"Maybe you shouldn't have said anything," he said, with a twinkle in his eyes. "That was your fault."

"How is it my fault?" I asked, a little peeved. "I didn't ask to nearly fall to my death. You're the one who knows this place and knew that we could fall in if we sat so close."

"There you go," he said with a gentle smile. "You can be mad at me."

He loosened his grip around my waist, and I realized that the adrenaline rush had faded in my annoyance. As I regained my balance, I looked up at him, and the sudden closeness made my heart beat faster. He was so close, yet I wanted to be even closer.

My hands rested on his chest and I could smell the comforting spice that was his cologne, stronger on him than on the hoodies he let me wear, and I took a deep breath, feeling his chest rise and fall with each breath that he took, wondering if he was going to let go but hoping that he wouldn't.

"I'm glad I was able to catch you," he said softly after a minute.

He looked down at my lips and the temperature between us rose—and so did my heart rate.

I'd told Keith I'd never been interested in kissing anyone before.

And now? That was no longer true.

Because I desperately wanted to kiss him.

I cleared my throat and took a step back, not sure what to do with this.

"Thank you for catching me," I said, unable to meet his eyes.

Somehow I knew if I looked, I would just want to kiss him even more.

"You're welcome," he said, his voice husky like he was just as affected by our closeness as I had been.

At least I wasn't alone.

"Shall we head back?"

Before I could answer him, there was a crash of thunder and we both looked up at the thin strip of sky we could see between the trees.

We hadn't noticed the storm clouds rolling in until it was too late.

"Yeah, I think it's time to go," I said with a grimace as the rain started. We could hear it hitting the trees and, soon enough, it was falling through, hitting us.

Keith led us down the trail towards the parking lot. "You know what they say in the Midwest: if you don't like the weather, wait ten minutes."

"We're gonna get soaked, aren't we?" I asked.

He chuckled as there was another crash of thunder, and he started moving faster. "Yeah, I think we're gonna get soaked. I guess we'll stop at the house so we can dry your clothes before your dad sees you."

"Probably a good idea." My father would not react well to the sight of me drenched.

Which is what I was quickly becoming.

By the time we made it to the parking lot, we were both drenched. As I climbed into the front seat of Keith's car, getting it totally wet in the process, I looked over at him and smiled to myself.

It had been such a fun afternoon, and I wanted to do it again. Wanted to see the waterfall with the hostas in bloom. Wanted to spend the afternoon in nature again.

Maybe someday, I'd be able to come back.

Maybe someday, I'd be able to have a relationship with someone like Keith.

Or maybe, if I could keep a secret from my dad, I could give in to the attraction between us and actually date Keith himself.

Maybe, just maybe, this could work.

Because every part of me wanted it.

Keith

There's nothing like walking into the house, soaked to the skin, with a girl who nobody in the family has met.

"Oh my goodness," Mom said, getting up from the table and hurrying over to us. "Hello, dear. Did you get stuck in the storm?"

"What do you think, Mom?" I asked with a laugh. "Of course we did."

"Well, let's get you dried off right away," Mom said. "I'll get you some of our clothes to wear while we put yours in the dryer." Then she took a closer look at Sarah and realized that the girl standing next to me was a lot taller than my sisters and mother and would probably never fit in their clothes.

"She can borrow something from me," I said. "Don't worry, I got it."

Everyone around the dining room table was staring and I knew that as soon as we walked out, they would be talking about us.

"Kait, do you mind if she uses your shower?" I asked.

"Not at all." Kaitlyn got up and followed us out of the dining room, shooting me a wide-eyed glance.

"Hi, I'm Kaitlyn," she said when we were safely in the hallway, away from the rest of the family.

I gestured to the soaking wet girl next to me. "This is Sarah."

This probably wasn't how she met a lot of people, her makeup mostly gone, her hair a mess, but she'd never looked more beautiful to me.

"Let me get you a clean towel," Kaitlyn said, grabbing one out of the hallway linen closet before ushering Sarah into her bedroom. "And I'll grab some clothes from Keith for you in a sec." Sarah looked at me and I nodded encouragingly before she disappeared into my sister's room. Kaitlyn would take good care of her.

I walked into my room and pulled out some basketball shorts and a patterned t-shirt. I'd heard my sisters complaining about not being able to wear regular t-shirts without a bra. And since I assumed her bra was soaking wet too, well, it made sense to give her something she could wear without it.

Just in case, I grabbed a sweatshirt too.

Underwear.

She probably needed underwear too.

Not that I had any.

But I grabbed a pair of boxers, though I had no idea if they'd fit her, or if she'd want to wear them.

I brought the stack to Kaitlyn's door, knocked, and waited for Kaitlyn to open it. She gave me a warning glance as she accepted the pile. "Stay here," she whispered before she disappeared, closing the door behind her.

This was the part where Kaitlyn chewed me out for not telling her that I was doing something with Sarah today.

I waited for my sister to reappear and was rewarded with a punch in the bicep when she did.

"You little sneak," she hissed as she closed the door behind her. "You didn't tell me she was coming."

"I didn't know she was," I said. "We got caught in the storm, so I had to dry her off before I took her back to the hotel."

"Yeah, well, you could have warned me. Where did you go, anyway?"

"I took her to the falls.'

"Oh man, I would have come with you," Kait whined.

"Maybe I wanted some alone time with her," I said.

Nope.

Damn it.

That came out wrong.

"No, not like that," I tried to say, but Kaitlyn was grinning like a fool and now there would be no stopping her.

"You wanted some alone time with her," she said in a singsong voice, drawing it out and poking me in the chest.

"Cut it out." I shoved her away. "I don't know what you're talking about."

"I know that my super serious brother hasn't stopped smiling since he showed up after getting caught in the rain with a gorgeous heiress."

"Shush," I said, looking around the hallway. "Nobody else knows."

"Nobody knows who she is?"

I shrugged. "I mean, this is the first time they've heard anything about her."

"Why wouldn't you tell them? Does she not want anyone to know?"

"I would imagine she doesn't want anyone to know."

"Really?" Kaitlyn looked skeptical. "She doesn't want anyone to know."

"I didn't actually ask her, but I doubt it."

"Maybe you should ask her. That seems kind of important."

I rolled my eyes at my sister. "I'm going to go shower. If she comes out before I'm done, don't let the others scare her off. Please."

Kaitlyn smiled. "Trust me. I'll take care of her for you."

I took one of the fastest showers of my life, and when I came back out of the bathroom wearing dry clothes, Sarah was just emerging from Kaitlyn's room, rubbing her wet hair with a towel.

The sight of her in my shorts and sweatshirt after the moment we'd shared earlier was nearly enough to make my heart stop. And the smile that she gave me didn't help, either.

"Feel better?" I asked.

"Well, I'm not as cold," she said. "You wouldn't happen to have a pair of socks though, would you? My feet are cold."

"Oh, yeah," I said, returning to my room and rifling through my sock drawer. When I turned around, Sarah was standing in the doorway looking over my room, which thankfully I had cleaned the night before.

"This is where you live?" she said.

"I know it's not much."

Her eyes took in my bedroom, which hadn't changed much since childhood, though I had removed the cartoon characters when I turned fifteen and thought I was a grown man.

"It's nice," she said. "It's very homey."

"Is homey an insult or a compliment?" I asked, not sure what the answer would be.

"It's a compliment. I like it."

"I'm glad my bedroom has your stamp of approval," I said with a grin. "It was something I was sorely missing in my life." She elbowed me and rolled her eyes. "Now, shall we go face the interrogation?"

Sarah grimaced. "They had no idea you were bringing a girl home, did they?"

I shrugged. "I don't care if they did or not. Either way, they're gonna tease me mercilessly as soon as you're gone... or maybe while you're still here."

"Sorry," she said, playing with a strand of her hair nervously.

"It's fine." I smiled at her, hoping to put her mind at ease. "I really don't mind. They only do it because they love me."

"It must be nice," she said softly. She looked away for a second and shook her head almost imperceptibly, squaring her shoulders and taking a deep breath before looking back at me.

"Are you ready?" I asked, offering my arm with a wink.

Sarah took my arm and sighed. "Ready as I'll ever be."

I led the way back into the heart of our home, where my family was waiting.

"Are you hungry?" Mom asked right away. "Dinner's hot."

I pulled up one of the extra chairs that we kept in the corner for unexpected guests and went to the kitchen for two plates as Sarah said, "I would love some food."

Dinner at the Palmer's' was served buffet-style, so I handed Sarah her plate and gestured to the kitchen counter, which was loaded with a pot of pasta, a big bowl of salad, a variety of salad dressings, and a covered plate, which must have been dessert. "Ladies and guests first," I said when she looked up at me. "Take what you want."

Sarah looked at the options and, as much as I didn't want to think about it, I was wondering if she'd ever had a family-style meal like this. I watched her load her plate with Mom's famous vodka pasta and warned, "There might be a little kick to the pasta. The sauce has vodka. Mom burned off the alcohol when we were kids, but now that we're all adults, she doesn't burn it all off the way she used to."

Technically Kathryn and Krystal weren't 21 yet, but there wasn't enough in the sauce for it to be an issue.

Mom grinned. "It tastes better with a little alcohol in it. Besides, it's how my family always made it."

"So, your family drinks then," Sarah said, turning around to look at Mom.

"Oh yes, but if yours doesn't, I have plenty of leftovers I can get in a jiffy," Mom said.

"No, no, no, I'm fine," Sarah said quickly as Mom started to get out of her seat. "I was just thinking out loud, sorry."

"I thought you would be okay with it." My mind flashed back to the margaritas I'd watched her down. From the way her face heated, I had a feeling she was thinking about them too. "But you never know. Sorry, I should have asked first."

"It's fine," she said, sitting down in what was normally my seat. I sat next to her in the chair I'd pulled up, my plate loaded with a pile of one of our family's favorite foods, and looked around in satisfaction. Having Sarah here felt right.

"Hi, everybody," Sarah said, since it was obvious that they were all staring at her. "I'm Sarah."

My siblings looked at each other and I knew where this was headed.

"I'm Kyle," our oldest brother said before they all stared at me expectedly.

I sighed. "I'm Keith."

"I'm Kaitlyn."

"I'm Kathryn."

"I'm Krystal."

We'd long since gotten used to introducing ourselves oldest to youngest, because if we didn't, everyone just got us confused. Not that the oldest to youngest thing made much of a difference since people still got confused, but they claimed it helped, so we were stuck doing it. Probably for the rest of our lives.

"That was us in oldest to youngest order," Krystal said helpfully.

"I see," Sarah said after swallowing a bite of food.

"I'm Natalie," Kaitlyn's best friend said from her seat next to Kait. "I live here with the Palmers."

"I'm Mr. Palmer, but you can call me Kevin if you want," my dad said.

"I'm Ashley, Kyle's girlfriend." Ashley was looking at Sarah with more interest than she should have. "You look familiar. Why do I recognize you?"

Sarah tensed beside me, and I shrugged. "Maybe you just have one of those faces that everybody recognizes," I said as an offhand comment to Sarah, hoping that would put Ashley off the trail.

But Ashley wouldn't be deterred. "No, no, I recognize you from somewhere. I just saw your face. Maybe on social media somewhere."

Sarah took a bite of her vodka pasta, ignoring Ashley's comment.

Kyle whispered something to Ashley.

Ashley harshly whispered something back.

There was a moment of awkward silence before Mom piped up. "So, how do you know Keith?" she asked.

Sarah looked at me in a moment of panic.

"We met at work," I said quickly, hoping that would be enough.

But unfortunately for me, Ashley was still on the idea that she knew Sarah.

"Oh, you met at the hotel? Do you work there too?"

"I was a guest," Sarah said, her shoulders tensing.

"You're allowed to fraternize with the guests?" Ashley asked me.

Beside me, Sarah was breathing faster and the realization that Ashley was making her anxious made me furious. What was she thinking, making someone uncomfortable in the Palmer house? She'd been Kyle's girlfriend long enough to know that making someone uncomfortable went against every part of the Palmer lifestyle.

But then again, Ashley had never cared too much about fitting in with the rest of the family.

Sensing the awkwardness, Mom cleared her throat and interrupted. "So Sarah, what were you and Keith doing that ended with you both looking like drowned rats?"

Sarah laughed. "We did look like a mess, didn't we? He took me to see the waterfall."

Couldn't she have said it in a way that didn't make it sound like we were together?

Now all of them were going to think I was dating her.

And yet, I didn't hate that idea, even as I knew that it was very much the wrong idea and would only lead to the teasing escalating as soon as she was gone.

"It was so beautiful until the moment the skies opened up," Sarah continued. "We did okay, though. We made it out alive."

"I'm grateful for that," Mom said. "We're a little attached to our Keith."

"Just a little?" I asked, looking around the table.

"I'm not," Kyle announced, and everyone laughed.

As we finished dinner, the conversation turned to which board games everyone wanted to play for family game night.

"We obviously have to play Bananagrams," Krystal said.

"What's that?" Sarah asked.

Everyone around the table stopped talking to stare between her and Krystal.

It was Krystal's favorite game, which meant that we spent a fair amount of time playing it. Not that any of us minded, since it was fun and easy. But not knowing what Bananagrams was seemed akin to murder in Krystal's eyes.

"How have you not heard of Bananagrams?" Krystal demanded. "It's, like, the best game ever."

"Well, you think it's the best game ever," I said.

"And now you get to introduce someone new to the joys of Bananagrams," Mom said soothingly, before Krystal could start ranting about it. Krystal had lots of opinions and was not shy about sharing them. "Now, who's ready for some key lime pie?"

Key lime pie was another Palmer family favorite. Did I forget someone's birthday or something? Why was she making everyone's favorites?

"Are we celebrating something?" Kathryn asked.

At least I wasn't the only one confused.

"We are celebrating the launch of my next set of group classes," Mom said with a huge smile. "I have a new series on birth trauma. The first one was today, and I think it was a huge success."

Everyone clapped and Mom sat there looking very proud of herself, as she should have been.

"So proud of you, honey," Dad said, leaning over to kiss her cheek. "You are an inspiration."

I looked around the table to see everyone agreeing with him. Mom was definitely an inspiration to all of us.

At least, all of her children.

I couldn't speak for Ashley or Sarah, though I knew Sarah already looked up to my mother. As for Ashley, well, she probably didn't care enough about anyone other than herself to look up to my mom.

After dessert, we cleaned up quickly and convened in the living room for game night. Kyle and I pulled out the card tables and the folding chairs, while the girls gathered the games and drinks for everyone. "How many are we?" Mom asked. "Nine? We can do one card game, or play some of the other games that everyone can play."

"Well clearly I have to learn how to play Bananagrams," Sarah said. "How many people is that?"

Krystal quickly claimed a seat at the Bananagrams table and I chose to sit there too, if only to keep Krystal from interrogating Sarah too much. Kat, Natalie, and Kait joined us, leaving Mom and Dad to play a card game with Ashley and Kyle, since Ashley had long since declared that she hated Bananagrams.

Sarah was instantly good at Bananagrams, which didn't surprise me. She probably learned lots of skills at her fancy heiress boarding school, and word games were probably right up her alley. To be honest, it didn't seem like she would have that much difficulty mastering anything.

We were just finishing our first game and dealing tiles for another when Ashley said triumphantly from across the room, "I knew it." Everyone turned to face her and she grinned at me, sending a chill down my spine, before she looked at Sarah. "I knew I recognized her from somewhere. You're Sarah Hanson, or should I say, Seraphina Hanson."

Sarah's face turned white and I reacted instantly.

"If she wanted everyone to know who she was, she would have told you," I said fiercely. "You had no right invading her privacy like this."

"It's on the internet," Ashley said, her mouth wide in a gloating smile. "It's public information, not invading her privacy at all."

"And again, she could have chosen to share that information with you if she wanted," I said.

"What are you doing here with Keith?" Ashley asked, turning to look at Sarah. "I mean, really? You could do better."

"That's enough," Kyle said, putting down his hand and getting to his feet. "It's time to go."

"I'm not ready to go," Ashley whined, "I have so many questions."

But Kyle wouldn't take no for an answer, taking her hand and pulling her to her feet. "Thank you for dinner, Mom," Kyle said. "It was nice to see all of you, and great to meet you, Sarah. I'm sorry."

Then he took his girlfriend and left.

Not for the first time, I was thankful for sibling loyalty.

"None of us like her anyway," Krystal said to Sarah as soon as the door closed behind them. "I'm sorry she did that to you."

"Me too," I said, turning to Sarah. "Are you okay?"

"I'm fine." She sounded tired and like she was about to cry, not like she was fine. "I just didn't want your family to think of me that way."

"Hey, if you just want to be treated like a normal person, you've come to the right place," Krystal said. "We'd probably treat royalty the same way we treat everyone else."

"Absolutely," Mom said, joining us at our Bananagrams table. "Whatever you want. We believe in always treating people the same around here, and that means treating them like they're family." Though the glare that she directed at the door said otherwise.

Sarah smiled at my family, who were all looking at her protectively. Who knew that Ashley would make my entire family be on Sarah's side? "Thank you," she said. "Ashley was right. My name is Sarah Hanson. My father owns the hotel that Keith works at, and he's been taking me to see all the sights that I don't normally get to see. He has been a huge blessing to me, and I am so thankful that I got to meet him and become his friend."

"I'm so glad that he's been good to you," Mom said, smiling at me. "You can parent as well as you can, but you never know how they behave when they're not at home."

"Well, you raised him wonderfully," Sarah said.

Dad spoke up, his tone dry. "Considering we have to put up with them, too, we decided raising our kids to be wonderful would be better than the alternative."

Sarah giggled. "You mean you didn't want to raise an asshole?"

"We already have one asshole hanging around," Krystal said, "no need for another one."

Mom gasped. "Krystal!"

"What? Everyone else is thinking it. I'm just the only one brave enough to say it."

"She might be right," I said.

Mom rolled her eyes. "It doesn't matter what other people do—"

"It does matter," Krystal said fiercely. "If people think they can come in here and treat people in this home with disrespect, we shouldn't be encouraging that, or encouraging them to come back. You have always made this home a place of respect and kindness, and how dare she desecrate this safe space?"

Mom sighed. "I agree with you, but there's nothing we can do about it now." Kaitlyn and Natalie shot each other a glance, obviously ready to disagree with her, and Krystal rolled her eyes.

"It's your home. I think you should talk to Kyle about it."

"Mom and Dad can decide if they want to do anything about it," Kathryn said, making the peace like she always did. "For now, let's get back to game night."

Dad nodded. "What Kathryn said. Sarah, you're welcome anytime you're in town, and we will treat you just like we treat everyone else if that's what you want."

Sarah grinned. "That is exactly what I want."

"You got it," Dad said with a tone of finality. And that was that. The topic was closed and everyone moved on.

Except for Krystal, who was still bent on vengeance.

"Still can't believe she said that," she muttered under her breath.

"Thank you for standing up for me," Sarah told her. "I appreciate it more than you know."

Krystal shrugged. "I stand up for anyone who Ashley bitches about—"

"Krystal, language," Mom said with a gasp.

"You don't even see half of it, Mom," Krystal whined. "She's better around you. Honestly, I'm surprised that she even said that much with you here. But I have to hear it constantly."

"Regardless of someone else's behavior, I will not have my daughter using such language. Now, if you're done, can we get back to playing?"

Krystal sighed, but ultimately, what Mom said went, so she had to stop griping and move on.

As the game resumed, it seemed most of us forgot there had been any unpleasantness at all, though Krystal was still muttering under her breath occasionally.

Even if I was still furious on Sarah's behalf, I was less likely to say something out loud than Krystal, and she'd already gotten the topic shut down.

Sarah spent the rest of the evening fitting in like she was part of the family. No one had become part of us this easily since we basically adopted Natalie when her father passed away. And it made me happy to watch my family treat Sarah like she was one of us, knowing how much it would mean to her.

But all too soon, I realized how late it was getting and that we were going to have a hard time making it back in time for Sarah's curfew. "I think we need to leave," I said, scooting my chair back from the table.

"No," Krystal whined, "please, not yet, I'm almost done beating Sarah again."

Sarah laughed. "Keith is right. I have to get back on time."

"You'll come back though, right?" Kathryn asked.

"If I can manage it," she said softly.

"You're always welcome here," Mom said, giving her a hug. "Trust me. I wouldn't say that if it wasn't true."

"Thank you," Sarah said as she melted into the hug.

How often did someone hug her, or show her even a scrap of affection? Her father certainly never did. I'd never met her mother, so I didn't know how affectionate she was, but I knew after growing up with my own mother how important touch was. She'd talked about study after study that showed how necessary physical affection was, and the emotional connections that it created. If Sarah didn't have any of that physical touch, it would explain why my family seemed so appealing to her. I didn't know what her day-to-day life was like, or how much of Sarah's actual life was reflected in the life she lived while she was traveling, but after meeting her father, it wasn't hard to imagine that she didn't have much affection in her life.

"Thank you for a wonderful evening." Sarah's voice caught as she let go of Mom. "I had an amazing time."

"We're almost always here, if you're ever in the area," Dad said, stepping next to Mom and resting his hand on her shoulder. "Hopefully you'll be able to stop by again."

"I would love that," Sarah said, smiling before looking at me. "We really do have to go, though."

"Let's get your clothes out of the dryer," I said, ushering Sarah towards the laundry room. If we didn't get out of here soon, we would actually be late. Sarah took her clothes from the dryer and I let her use my bathroom to change, smiling when I noticed the neatly folded pile of my clothing that she left behind as I followed her towards the front door.

By the time we made it into the car, we were definitely late, but I was enjoying the evening too much to care. Shortsighted, maybe, but it had been an incredible evening.

I looked over at her as I drove away from home. "Well, did my family scare you? I know they can be pretty intimidating."

"Your family is wonderful," she said softly, looking off into the distance. "I wish my family were more like yours."

I didn't know what to say, so I didn't say anything.

"You're very lucky," she added after a minute, looking back at me. "You know that?"

"I know," I admitted. "I wish everyone could have a family like mine."

"Me too."

In the silence that followed, I let my hand rest in the middle of the console, palm up. As much as I wanted to reach for her, to offer some small physical comfort, I wasn't going to be the one to breach that barrier. But it was there, if she wanted to take that step.

She glanced over and her breath caught, so quiet I almost didn't hear it. Out of the corner of my eye, I saw her fingers flexing as she debated whether or not to take my hand.

I made the decision easier, sliding my arm closer.

If she'd been any other girl, I would have already reached over and laced my fingers through hers. But she wasn't just any girl. She was Sarah Hanson, heiress to the Hanson fortune, and my boss's daughter. I couldn't just hold her hand... could I?

But then again, after everything I'd already done with her, was crossing this boundary any worse?

I took her hand in mine before I could change my own mind again, and the tiny smile that appeared on her face made every moment of concern worth it.

"Thank you for letting me borrow your family for an evening," she said, smiling over at me. "Your mom made me feel so welcome, and your siblings are great, and your dad didn't say much but I like him too. And the food was delicious, and your mom gave me a hug, and it was... it was one of the best evenings I've had in a very long time."

I was gonna hug my mom extra hard before I went to bed tonight.

If our family evening chaos was one of the best evenings she'd had, what would an evening without any Ashley unpleasantness be like?

And what would her evenings be like now that she was going back home?

The silence turned melancholy as I wondered what my evenings might be like without my family.

In an effort to brighten the mood that had suddenly grown somber, I turned to look at her and said, "So. Seraphina."

She blushed and shook her head. "I should have known that you'd pick up on that. Yes, it's Seraphina. My mom's one and only act of rebellion. It's too whimsical for my dad, of course, so I go by Sarah. But yes, if you wanted to tease me, you could call me Seraphina."

I thought about it for a moment, my face exaggerating the thinking. "I think you're more of a Phee than a Seraphina."

Her nose wrinkled. "Phee?"

"Yeah, I think so."

"And why is that?" she asked.

I shrugged. "I don't know, you just seem like a Phee to me."

Did I actually have a reason for it? Nope. But it seemed enough to make her smile.

"Maybe that can be your nickname for me. You can be the only person who calls me that. It'll be different."

"I don't mind being different. Only if it's a good different, though."

She smiled. "It's good."

I glanced over at her, the tension between us so thick you could cut it with a knife. What was I doing? Holding her hand, giving her a nickname? That was boyfriend stuff. I wasn't her boyfriend, and I wasn't going to be. But I couldn't make myself let go.

I cleared my throat. Time for a new topic. Something less personal than nicknames. Something distracting. "So, what did you really think of Bananagrams?" I asked. "Were you just saying that you enjoyed it to appease Krystal?"

"No, it was fun. It reminded me of Scrabble, but easier and faster."

"So much easier, especially when you're playing with my siblings, who are far too competitive for their own good."

She grinned. "I liked your siblings."

We didn't talk about Ashley.

She probably didn't want to, and I didn't really want to either. None of us really knew why Kyle was still dating her, or what had happened that turned her from the girl we used to know into a bitter woman who didn't know when to let things go. But until she changed, or Kyle broke up with her, we were stuck with her.

I didn't want to think about Ashley, much less discuss her with Sarah, so I turned the radio on and we drove in silence for a little bit. When I looked over again, Sarah had fallen asleep, still holding my hand. I enjoyed my chance to sneak a peek—or three—without her noticing.

She was the most beautiful girl I knew. She had changed back into her clothes, and yet she still wore my hoodie. The sight of her wearing something of mine made me smile.

Even though I shouldn't feel anything at the sight of her wearing my sweatshirt, because she wasn't mine.

The thought was harder to stomach every time I had it.

I let her sleep the rest of the way to the city, but pulled over and called a cab when we were a few blocks from the hotel. There was no need for anyone at the hotel to see her getting out of my car.

"Sarah, hey," I said softly when I hung up, squeezing her hand, which was still holding mine. She would probably want a minute to wake up before getting into the cab.

"Where are we?" she asked, sitting bolt upright and yanking her hand out of mine, looking around in confusion.

"I called a cab to take you the rest of the way," I said. "It will be here in a minute."

"That's smart," she said, relaxing into the seat again with a yawn. "Sorry for falling asleep."

"Hey, it's dark and you've had a long day," I said. "If I weren't driving, I would've fallen asleep too."

She smiled. "Thank you for a wonderful day, Keith. That was the most fun I've had in a very, very long time."

"Maybe next time you come, we can do something again," I said quietly. I shouldn't even put the idea into her head, but I was already thinking about when I could see her again.

"I would like that," she said as a cab pulled up and parked in front of us. She opened the door. "Goodbye, Keith."

She closed the door before I could reply. I watched her get into a cab, waited for it to pull away, and turned around to drive home.

It wasn't until I got home and gave my mom a hug, listened to Krystal tell me that she liked Sarah better than she liked Ashley, and realized that Sarah still had my sweatshirt, that I realized just how much I wanted this to be real.

How much I wanted her to be mine.

Sarah

My heart beat fast as I made my way through the hotel lobby a few minutes after my eight o'clock curfew. Would Dad be back in the room yet? He wasn't usually back by now, but maybe he'd come back early to see if I'd made it back in time.

I hurried into our suite and was relieved to hear silence, but there was no guarantee that he wasn't in his bedroom, so I went to my room quickly and closed the door. Breathing a slight sigh of relief, I took my shoes off and was shimmying out of my jeans when I heard the outer suite door opening.

I was usually reading in bed when Dad got back.

Crap.

Running and jumping into bed with my clothes on, I pulled the covers up to my chin, hoping Dad wouldn't notice that I was still wearing full makeup if he came in.

If he didn't, we would be good.

There was a knock on my bedroom door and I called, "Come in," barely half a second before Dad stuck his head in. "Hello," I said.

"I just wanted to make sure you remember that we have brunch tomorrow."

I nodded, trying not to let my face show how much I didn't want to see Julian.

"I expect you to make a good impression."

When did he not expect me to make a good impression?

I waited for him to leave, knowing he didn't want to hear me actually say anything.

"I'll be in meetings the rest of the day," he said, "so I expect you to make sure you come straight back to the hotel."

Of course.

"Yes, sir," I said.

He left, closing the door loudly, and I climbed back out of bed with a sigh and went to the bathroom to get ready for bed.

I didn't realize I was still wearing Keith's sweatshirt until I saw it in the mirror. I pulled the collar to my nose to sniff it, the faint smell of Keith and his cologne making me smile.

I wore the sweatshirt to bed. I knew it was foolish. But I couldn't make myself leave it in the bathroom.

The next thing I knew, the sun was shining, even though I had no recollection of falling asleep whatsoever. Apparently I'd been super tired.

I stretched in bed, realizing how sore I was after hiking the falls the day before. As much as I didn't like being sore, the reminder of the amazing day that I'd had made me smile.

It had been a good night of sleep, too. I couldn't think of how long it had been since I'd slept so well.

It felt later than normal, too.

Wait.

I looked at my watch.

9:57.

Oh no.

I sprang out of bed, yanking Keith's sweatshirt off as I ran, and got dressed and did my makeup in record time, meeting my father in the common room just as he was walking out of his bedroom.

"How did you sleep?" I asked politely, though he never really answered. This morning's response was more of a grunt, which was fine by me.

If he didn't answer, I didn't have to say anything.

We didn't speak on our way to brunch, which gave me even more time to think about yesterday, and how much fun I'd had, and how wonderful it was to spend time with people who loved each other.

Watching Mr. and Mrs. Palmer together was almost difficult, because I had never gotten to see a marriage like that, a marriage that was loving and sweet and supportive.

My parents were always cold with each other.

It was hard to think about everything that I had lost due to the family I had, but there was nothing I could do about it. I had been born into a family where the parents barely tolerated each other—my father was cold and distant, and my mother was withdrawn and silent to survive dealing with him—and that was my life.

So when I'd spent an evening with a family like the Palmers, well... it was probably best to not think about it too much, because my life was unlikely to turn out that way.

As much as I wanted it to turn out that way.

As much as I wanted to cling to the Palmers so hard that they could never let go, whether they wanted to or not.

A family like that wasn't in my future.

Most, if not all, of the men in my world weren't capable of creating a family like them.

I wanted to believe that if it was possible for them, surely I could try to create it on my own. But when we walked into brunch, there was Julian leering at me from a table, and my good mood evaporated.

No, a supportive, loving family didn't seem possible in my future.

Julian pulled out a chair for me, his fingers lingering on the back to brush against my shoulders before he sat down across from me, his feet venturing across the distance to touch mine.

I didn't know how my father knew his—I forgot those details quickly now. My father had questionable taste in friends, which led to questionable sons, and they all wanted to be with me. Julian was only one of many and, unfortunately, was one of the more physical of them. Nothing too over the top, but all of it just enough to make me uncomfortable.

I tried to pay attention as Julian started a conversation—that was more like a monologue— about horse racing and the probably millions of dollars that they had spent on it.

What was I doing, sitting here listening to him when it was the last thing I wanted to do? Really, I just wanted to be anywhere else.

But I sat in silence and listened to him talk about pedigrees and race times for horses that I'd never heard about and had no interest in hearing about.

What was I supposed to do? I could only fake an interest for so long. Probably not long enough to get to the end of this conversation.

"Sarah," my father barked, and I realized that I'd zoned out for a bit.

Uh oh.

"Sorry, what was that?" I asked, avoiding my father's gaze as Julian repeated his question, asking if I'd ever been to a horse race, which I had not. "No, I haven't had the pleasure."

"I'll have to take you to one," Julian said, sounding very confident in his ability to take me somewhere. Did he and my father already have plans that I didn't know about?

Ugh. Dad was definitely going to lecture me later, and I deserved it for letting my mind wander. I knew better than that. Dad wanted me on my best behavior every time I met someone, whether it was a client or someone he was trying to set me up with. Julian having to repeat his question would be viewed as the ultimate insult on my part, by my father at least.

But one of these days, I was going to stop listening altogether. Any part of my brain that was capable of listening to men prattle on about subjects that didn't interest me was quickly dying a miserable death.

Probably brought on by the fact that I'd started talking to someone who I actually enjoyed spending time with.

"Are you listening, Sarah?" Dad asked. "I would hate for you to not be paying attention."

At the not so subtle threatening tone in his voice, a chill ran down my spine.

What did that mean? He'd never said anything like that before. Was he losing patience with me and my reluctance to commit to someone? Was I running out of time before he would make me choose?

I didn't know, but suddenly I was anxious.

"Of course," I said with a smile. "I'm sorry, I was thinking about horse racing and how I've never been involved in it, but it seems so interesting. I loved reading about horses when I was growing up."

Dad gave me a severe look but went back to talking to Julian's father.

I had to check back into this conversation, or my lack of interest was going to lead me to trouble.

"What does your family do for charity?" I asked Julian in an effort to actually contribute to this conversation.

Julian laughed.

He actually laughed about it.

I didn't realize that charity was a laughing matter. I'd briefly talked to Mrs. Palmer about it the night before and she'd been so interested.

I should have realized that some people would not have the same reaction, should have known Julian well enough to realize that he would be one of them.

I suppose it wasn't that unusual for a man in our world to not care about charity, that was the women's work, but to actually laugh about it?

It was the best part of what I did, the best part of the life that I led, and for him to act that way hurt. Even though it shouldn't have, even though I should have known better, even though I should've known that trying to engage Julian in a conversation about something important to me wasn't worth it.

Whatever.

Julian's reaction wasn't that important.

But after spending an evening with Keith's family, what had seemed so normal to me suddenly felt dull and awful, and all I could do was wish that I was with the Palmers instead.

What would my life be like if I didn't have to spend most of it in the company of people who didn't care about me or my opinions?

"It's time to go, Sarah," my father said, interrupting my thoughts with a cold voice. "Come along."

I dutifully pushed back my chair, collected my purse, and stood. Julian followed my lead, then stepped closer and leaned in for a kiss. My heart stopped and I slipped sideways out of his grasp, his lips just brushing against my cheek as I moved. I shivered involuntarily as I realized that Julian had just tried to kiss me.

He'd tried to kiss me. After laughing at me when I tried to talk to him.

He could have been aiming for my cheek, but it wasn't likely.

I tried to avoid the murderous look that my father gave me, but I knew I'd made enough mistakes during one brunch that he would be giving me a talk later.

"It was lovely to see you," I said, clutching my purse like a shield. "I hope you all have a wonderful game of golf." I nodded to my father, turned around, and walked out of the restaurant.

Or at least, I started to. I didn't make it far before my father caught up to me and grabbed my elbow tightly. "What was that?" he said, his voice harsh.

I glanced at the waiters standing by the door, who were both carefully avoiding my gaze.

I wasn't getting any help from them.

"Nothing," I said. "I thought you were all ready to leave for golf."

"It wasn't nothing," he said, his voice tight with displeasure. He flagged down a cab and handed me in. "I will talk to you later," he said, and I prayed that this would be one of the golf outings where he would drink so much that he forgot his threat.

I collapsed into the seat as the cab drove back to the hotel, my fingers rubbing my cheek where Julian's lips had touched me.

As soon as I got back, I was going to scrub my face.

Thinking about the disastrous brunch sent chills down my spine. Could it have gone any more wrong?

As we pulled up, I was still anxious about my father and his reaction to me sidestepping Julian's kiss. What would he say when he got back?

I was going to puke, and not just from the motion sickness in the back of the cab.

I opened the cab door and stepped out, taking a deep breath before walking through the doors. I was prepared to head straight to the penthouse, but then I saw Keith at the front desk.

Keith.

Just seeing him made my legs weak with relief.

When he noticed me, his eyes lit up. "May I help you with anything, Miss Hanson?"

"I think I'm going to sit at the bar for a little while," I said in a moment of rebellion. I was expected to stay in the room, but it wasn't leaving the room if I'd never made it up there, right?

"Let me know if I can get you anything," Keith said.

His smile was almost enough to distract me from all the anxiety of earlier, but what I really wanted was for him to come sit with me at the bar.

He probably wouldn't be allowed to do that, though.

"Actually, I changed my mind. I'm going to go to my room. Would you carry this for me?"

Keith smiled as I handed over my bag of leftovers. It made me feel slightly ridiculous, handing off such a small bag, but it was the only excuse I could think of to get him to come with me.

The ride up the elevator was quiet. Since we were alone, I turned to Keith, but he shook his head almost imperceptibly, glancing up at the ceiling, where I noticed a security camera staring at us.

Okay then, nothing until we were safely in the penthouse.

He followed me into the penthouse, setting the leftovers down on the side table.

"Are you okay?" he asked, taking a step closer to me.

"I don't know," I said softly, wrapping my arms around myself.

"What happened?"

I shrugged. "I don't even know."

Keith reached out and took my hand, pulling me gently to the couch and settling me there, fetching a blanket and arranging it on my lap before sitting next to me, though not close enough to touch. "Why don't you start at the beginning?" he suggested.

"We were at brunch," I said slowly, the words sticking in my throat. "I was having a horribly dull time, and the young man my father was trying to set me up with was being awful—some people would say he was being kind of douchey—and then he tried to kiss me as we were leaving, and I shut down and my father is furious with me, and I don't know what to do or what's going to happen, and I just—"

The panic started to clog my airway and suddenly breathing was too difficult and maybe I'd just die before my father came back, that might be easier than dealing with him, and—

"Hey, it's okay." Keith reached over and took my hands in his, rubbing circles on the insides of my wrists with his thumbs. "I'm right here. Take a deep breath with me." I took deep breaths with him, allowing the panic and the nausea to settle.

He made me feel safe.

"I just felt so gross," I whispered when I could breathe again. "Like the only reason I was there was for him to make a move on me, and our fathers expected it and were just going to let it happen. The waiters wouldn't even look at me... I've never felt so trapped. I didn't want him to kiss me. I don't want anyone else to kiss me, only—"

I froze, realizing what I was about to say.

The only person I wanted to kiss me was Keith.

He was the only man I'd ever spent time with who saw me, who was interested in the real me, who cared about me and my interests, not just my money and the fact that I would be the perfect society wife.

"Only what?" Keith asked quietly, tracing the outside edge of each of my fingers with his index finger slowly, a soothing movement.

"Nothing," I said sheepishly.

The corner of his mouth perked up. "Nothing, huh? I'm glad you weren't about to say something about only wanting a certain someone to kiss you... not that I would judge you for that."

I blushed harder than I'd ever blushed in my life. "Am I that obvious?" I whispered.

"Only because I feel the same way," he said softly.

The longing that I'd felt before returned like a waterfall, drenching me like a pop-up rainstorm.

I slid closer, knowing that if he went for it, I wouldn't stop him.

He leaned in and my heart stopped beating, in a good way this time.

His arm came around my waist, pulling me close.

Every part of me felt alive.

And then he turned away, letting go and putting space between us, my heart free falling in the space he left.

"I can't," he said.

If it wouldn't have been even more embarrassing than him refusing to kiss me, I would have burst into tears.

"It's not you," he said, shaking his head at me. "Don't even think it for a minute. I know you, Phee, I can see those wheels turning in your head."

"Is it the job? Because I could do something."

"It's not the job," he said. "But I'm not going to be the man who makes you break your vow, no matter how much we both want it."

The softness in his eyes was the thing that ultimately made me cry. He cared that much about the vow that I'd made years ago, that I'd briefly mentioned once?

"You probably have a lot of men in your life who want to kiss you, and they may not care about your boundaries, but I respect you too much to be the man who carries you past them." He stood and took a step back. "Can I do anything else for you, Miss Hanson?"

The distance that he put between us by calling me Miss Hanson hurt more than anything.

"Well, I'd do just about anything for a foot rub right now, but I suppose that's probably outside of normal bellhop duties," I joked, trying to keep my tone light to distract from how much I was hurting.

He thought about it for a moment, indecision warring on his face. "I suppose that might be allowed," he said finally, sitting back down and gesturing for me to put my feet in his lap, "although I could probably call a masseuse, they would do a better job."

I rolled my eyes at him as I kicked my heels off and lifted my legs, resting my feet on his thigh. I sighed in relief as his hands started to work their magic. "You're good at this," I said. "You sure you're not a masseuse?"

"Pretty sure I'm not," he said with a grin. "Although my mom has made me practice a lot."

I relaxed into the couch as he rubbed the tension out of my feet. Somehow, this moment seemed far more intimate than the moment before when he'd almost kissed me. Closing my eyes, it was far too easy to imagine coming home to Keith every day, snuggling up on the couch together and getting the occasional foot rub.

My phone buzzed, startling me from my fantasy.

I took a deep breath as I read it.

"Everything okay?" Keith asked.

"Apparently, we're leaving early. Dad wants me to pack my things."

Keith frowned. "Are you going to be okay?"

"He won't hurt me," I said when I realized what Keith's concern was. "He'll be grumpy and mad, but hopefully he'll be too busy with whatever it is that has us leaving early to give me a lecture."

Keith sighed. "I should probably go before he gets here. You're sure you'll be all right?"

"I'll be fine," I said. "It was good to see you. Thank you. For everything." My voice caught in my throat and I hoped that he knew I meant more than just the foot rub.

"I'm here if you need me. You know I'm only a phone call away."

I tried to laugh, but it came out more like a sob. "And a plane ride."

"I've heard it doesn't take long if you have a private jet," he said with a wink.

"We'll be back for an acquaintance's wedding in two weeks," I said. "Will I be able to see you?"

"I'll do my best to be here," he said, moving as if he were getting ready to stand. I swung my feet off his lap and he reached over for my hand, taking it and kissing the back of it. "Be careful, Phee."

Then he stood and let himself out of the room without looking back.

I sat there on the couch for a minute with my eyes closed, relishing the moment we'd just shared for just a minute longer. But then I stood and locked myself in my bedroom to start putting things in my suitcase, because what happened when I was with Keith didn't matter. What mattered was what Dad saw and how that affected the rest of the day.

And today, he was going to be miserably grumpy.

So I'd pack, and I'd get ready to leave, and then I'd think about stolen moments and foot rubs until I got home.

December

Phee: *Just so you know, doing a puzzle with my mom is boring after Palmer game night.*
7:24 pm

We've spoiled you for anything else, hmm?
7:26 pm

Phee: *There's a lot less fun, a lot more serious musing about finding corner pieces.*
7:32 pm

I bet Krystal could make corner piece musings funny.

7:33 pm

Phee: *OMG, please record that and send it to me, I'm dying to hear it now.*

7:47 pm

Your wish is my command. Check your snaps, my lady

;)

8:15 pm

Friday, December 2nd

What would you do if I called in sick this weekend?

9:22 am

Phee: *Are you sick??*

9:22 am

No, I just wondered how mad you'd be.
9:24 am

Phee: *Jerk.*
9:25 am

You still coming back today?
9:26 am

Phee: *Yup, one of dad's friend's has a kid getting married tomorrow.*
9:28 am

I'm not working today, if you can manage to get out.
9:36 am

Phee: *I'll try. If not, see you tomorrow?*
9:28 am

Definitely. :)
9:36 am

Sarah was coming back today and, for some reason, I was nervous about it.

I wasn't sure what had changed. We'd been texting, but that shouldn't have been enough to make me nervous. Maybe it was the sudden realization that everything was changing and Sarah would have to make a choice soon.

And no matter how much we wished it, I was not one of the choices.

I knew that, even though I continued to ignore it.

My family was worried about me, at least Mom and Kaitlyn were, and I knew they thought I was being stupid for continuing to spend time with her. But I couldn't abandon her now. She needed a friend and I needed a reason to smile, and for the time being, we could fill those voids for each other.

It was gonna be fine.

I could spend time with her without getting too attached, because I was an adult who could control his emotions.

My family was worrying for no reason.

I glanced at my phone as I drove, waiting for a text from Sarah to pop up, letting me know whether she could get out or not. I was driving all the way to the city without knowing, but I didn't have much homework to do and it was a nice day out, and hey, I could work on homework in the park if she couldn't get away. The sun was shining, and it was warm enough for December that I had my windows cracked as I sang along to the country song on the radio.

I never listened to country music until her. This was her fault.

A text popped up and I glanced down at my phone. *Mom's napping, see you soon.* I grinned and sent back a thumbs up.

Apparently her mom came for weddings.

The plan was to go to a park and hang out. I had a picnic basket, a blanket, and a Bluetooth speaker in my trunk, which made it feel rather like a date.

But it wasn't a date. It couldn't be.

It was just friends hanging out.

As I came around the corner towards work, I pulled into the employee parking and stopped in my usual spot.

Should I walk around and wait for her? I didn't want to sit in my car like a loser, and I also didn't want it to look bad if someone from work came and saw me sitting there, since we weren't supposed to use the parking lot when we weren't working.

I got out of my car, pulling out the picnic basket, and began walking towards the front of the building. I could meet her a block or two down the street.

I was halfway around the building when I saw someone climbing down the fire escape. Who was that idiot?

Probably some dumbass kid showing off or sneaking out.

I wasn't clocked in. It wasn't my problem.

I rolled my eyes and kept walking, but paused and looked up one more time.

Sneaking out.

There was no way Sarah was stupid enough to try climbing down the fire escape, right?

And yet, before she got down to the last landing, I could tell it was her.

She pushed down the drop ladder and started to climb down it, definitely not realizing that it was stuck halfway. "Sarah," I yelled, racing forward the last thirty feet to stand underneath her, like I would be able to catch her. "What the hell are you doing?"

She looked down, clinging to the ladder as she reached the last extended rung.

"What does it look like I'm doing?" she asked. "Why doesn't it go all the way down?"

"It must be rusty or something," I said, setting down the basket and reaching up to see if I could reach her, though she was still way too far above my head. When had the fire escapes last been inspected? "I can't believe you did this."

"Well, Mom's asleep in the living room," she said, looking down at me with a wrinkled nose. "I couldn't sneak out that way without waking her up."

"I assume that means you won't go back up and come down the elevator like a sane person?"

She shook her head. "I'm this close to freedom. I'm not blowing it now."

I groaned. "If you can climb down a bit more and hang from your arms, I could probably grab around your knees, but you'd have to keep them locked until I get you down."

"You better not let go of me," she warned, lowering herself by her arms, her feet leaving the safety of the final rung.

I watched, my heart in my throat as she hung there, dropping herself down slowly, rung by rung, her toes pointing towards me.

It was agonizingly slow.

As she came within reach, I put my hands on her feet, then her ankles, sliding my way up to her knees, her jeans sliding up as I tried to take as much of her weight as I could.

"If you ever do this again, I'm going to kill you," I said.

"I don't think you have to worry about that." She was breathing heavily as she hung off the last rung, my hands firmly supporting the backs of her thighs. "Catch me."

She let go and I tensed as all of her weight suddenly landed on me. I tried to control her descent, sliding her down my torso, every nerve in my body on fire. She laced her arms around my neck and hung on, grinning. "Well, that was fun."

I glared at her. "That was not fun, and if you ever do it again, you are dead. I'm serious."

"Nice to see you too," she said with a saucy smirk, flipping her ponytail and stepping away from me.

"You are ridiculous. What would you have done if I hadn't been there to catch you?"

"I would have climbed back up, but you did catch me. I knew you would."

I ran my fingers through my hair, groaning. "Your father would have killed me if you'd gotten hurt."

"Well, I don't know that he would have killed you, but he definitely would have sued you within an inch of your life."

"That's so reassuring, thank you."

"You're welcome," she said, looking up at me with a grin.

I sighed and picked up the picnic basket. "Come on, let's get out of here before you decide to come up with another harebrained decision that'll kill one of us."

"That's not fair," she protested. "I haven't killed anybody yet."

"Was that before or after you decided to climb out the window?"

"We have a balcony," she informed me, tossing her hair.

"You still climbed over your balcony to get onto the fire escape."

Silence.

"That's what I thought. Now, do you want to walk or drive?"

"Where are we going?" she asked.

"There's a park a few blocks from here where I thought we could hang out, since it's nice out today. But if it's too cold for you, we can go somewhere else."

She shook her head. "I'll be fine. It's a little colder than I'm used to, but it's not too bad, and I've got this." She shrugged her shoulder at me, showing off a thin, lacey cardigan.

I frowned. What was the average temperature in California in December? Probably not the chilly weather that we had now. "I have a feeling that's not gonna be enough. Let's stop at my car and grab an extra sweatshirt for you, just in case."

"You think so?" she asked, clutching it around her shoulders. "I feel okay for now."

"'For now' being the key words, right after you just climbed down seventeen floors of fire escape. We don't want to have to come back in five minutes because you can't handle the cold."

"Hey, I'm tougher than I look," she protested. But when we got to my car, she willingly accepted my extra hoodie and pulled it on.

"Now are you ready?" I asked, picking up the picnic basket and blanket.

"I am," she said as she reached for my free hand.

Before I could think about it, I pulled away, and then I noticed the hurt in her eyes. "We're still really close to the hotel," I said quietly, hoping the explanation would help, but all it did was make her look away from me.

"I don't care," she said softly. She took a step away from me, her voice catching as she said, "I understand if you don't want to risk it, though."

The hurt in her voice was almost physically painful for me. All I wanted to do was wrap my arms around her. What were the chances of someone seeing us? Probably higher than I wanted to think about. But I couldn't stand to see her so upset because of me, so I reached over and took her hand.

Her smile was wide enough to light up the whole world.

I would give anything to see that smile every day.

Well shit, that was a strange thought.

I led the way to the park, her hand warm in mine. She babbled non-stop the whole time we walked, and I did my best to pay attention, but my mind was busy with other things.

Specifically, why she affected me so much. Why I was so emotionally invested in seeing her smile. Why I was willing to risk my job, my career, to make her happy.

Was it worth losing everything for these smiles and these stolen moments?

Did I even want to know the answer to that question?

It wasn't until we were settling on the picnic blanket and opening the basket, and I watched Sarah squeal with delight when she saw the makeshift charcuterie that I'd brought in various containers, that I realized yes, it was worth it.

The afternoon passed too quickly as we sat on the picnic blanket like we were a normal couple, talking, eating fruit and cheese, laughing, and listening to quiet music on my speaker.

An old couple walking the path smiled fondly at us and Sarah sighed. "I love seeing older couples who are clearly in love," she said. "I always wondered what it must be like to have a relationship like that."

I watched them walk away, holding hands and smiling as they talked to each other.

My parents had a relationship like that and I'd always assumed that I would have one too.

Sarah probably hadn't ever seen a relationship like that, much less thought that she would be able to have one.

"I wish things could be different for you," I said after a minute.

Sarah laid down on the blanket, staring up at the blue sky. "I wish that too, but I don't think it's meant to be. I'll just have to keep stealing my moments with you and enjoy them while it lasts." She looked up at me with a grin. "But what about you? Is your plan to find someone and grow old together and have lots of beautiful children?"

She seemed to realize after asking that she didn't actually want to know the answer, because she looked away and frowned.

My stomach clenched. Was she wondering what it would be like if we could be together? If we were the ones growing old together and having lots of beautiful children?

I decided to spare her emotions. "I don't know. I never really thought about it."

It was a lie, and the look on her face told me she knew that, but hopefully it didn't make her hurt any more than she already did.

We'd been sitting there talking for almost three hours when my stomach growled. Apparently, the snacks that I'd brought hadn't been enough. "Should you get back?" I asked, "Or can we sneak out to dinner?"

She grimaced. "I should probably head back, but I don't want to go yet."

"Dinner it is," I said. The smile on her face let me know I'd made the right choice. "Where do you want to go?" I asked.

"Somewhere that's not fancy, but other than that, I don't care." She shrugged. "Take me somewhere that my dad would be horrified to go."

Not fancy and horrifying to her father? I could do that. Only a couple of blocks away was one of my favorite restaurants, a little hole-in-the-wall Greek place that served gyros, baklava, and more. I wasn't entirely sure what the "and more" was, since I pretty much just got gyros and baklava, but if she didn't like those, I was sure she could find something else on the menu.

When we walked into the place, her eyes lit up. "This is amazing," she said, taking a deep breath and looking around, her eyes wide. "I never get to go to places like this."

"What would you like?" I asked, gesturing to the menu. "I like their lamb gyro."

"Oh, no, this is my treat." She pulled her wallet out of her purse. "You took care of lunch."

I shrugged but let her walk up to the counter before me.

"What do I want?" she asked me.

"Have you ever had a gyro before?"

"Never," she said, scanning the menu. "Why don't you order for both of us? It smells so good, I'm sure I'll like anything. Get a couple things that I can try."

I stepped up and rattled off an order—a chicken gyro, a lamb gyro, a side of falafel, an order of spanakopita, an order of pita with hummus and tzatziki, and both a chocolate baklava and a regular one.

"I don't know what any of that is, but it sounds amazing," Sarah said as we found seats in a corner booth, tucked in the back of the restaurant.

"How have you never had Greek food before?" I asked. "It's one of the most incredible things in the world and I can't believe that I get to be the one to introduce you to it."

"If it's not served in French restaurants or by fancy catering companies, I probably haven't had it."

"You poor, spoiled child," I said, grinning at her to soften my words, though this was only one more reminder of the differences between us. "We have to fix this immediately."

"I'm looking forward to it," she said, looking around with a smile.

When our food arrived, I rearranged the tray in front of her, pointing everything out and naming it all as I did. "This is a chicken gyro. The white sauce on it is a Greek sauce called tzatziki, with cucumber and dill and yogurt. We have a side of it over here, with pita and hummus, so you can dip if you need more. This is falafel, a fried snack, and these pie-ish things are spanakopita, which is a spinach and feta pie. They're my dad's favorite. And these baklava are for dessert, so we'll save those."

I watched as she took her first bite of Greek food. Sarah groaned in delight as the flavors must have exploded in her mouth. "This is so good," she said around a full mouth.

It was so good apparently that she forgot her manners, something I didn't get to see often. "I told you."

"Oh my gosh, how have I never had this before?"

"Isn't that what I just said?"

She grinned for half a second before shoveling another bite into her mouth. With her enjoying it, I settled in to eat my own food, but then realized she'd probably never had lamb that wasn't served in whatever way the French prepared it, so she probably didn't know anything about real gyro meat.

"You should try mine," I said, holding it over the table for her. She quickly swallowed and leaned over to take a bite, her eyes growing wide as she chewed and swallowed.

"How is that even better than mine?" She looked at mine, then looked at hers.

"We can trade," I said after a second as she continued to stare.

"Oh, I mean, we don't have to. I can go get another one."

"Just take the gyro, Phee."

I laughed as she eagerly traded.

The chicken gyro definitely wasn't as good as the lamb, but the sacrifice was worth it. I would have gyros again soon, but Sarah might not for a very long time.

We ate in silence for a while before Sarah sighed, staring down at the food. "This is so good. I don't know why my dad never lets us go to restaurants that aren't fancy."

"I don't know why your dad doesn't let you do a lot of things. His reasons don't make any sense to me."

"You have no idea. I haven't even told you half of it. You'd probably just get upset like my other friends."

"Why do your other friends get upset?" I asked, dread settling in my stomach. What wasn't she telling me? And more importantly, what were the things that she wasn't telling anyone? What parts did she bury in shame and refuse to tell anyone for fear of their reaction?

Those were the dangerous parts.

"I don't know—it's mostly little things," she said.

"Like what?"

"Well, he likes to brag about me, but never to me. He'll brag about me to all of his friends and loves listening to them talk about how amazing I am. But he never gives me a scrap of praise himself. And you know he's controlling. You've probably seen that more than my other friends. And they just don't like it."

"If your friends don't like it, there's probably a reason," I said softly. "You deserve better."

"I know." She sighed.

"Just because he's your father doesn't mean he's allowed to mistreat you. If anything, it means he absolutely shouldn't, because he should be the one standing between you and the world."

She looked down at her gyro, swallowing hard.

If I kept talking about this, it would just make her sad, and there was nothing we could do about it right now. "Why don't you finish that gyro and you can try baklava for the first time," I said, setting it in front of her.

Her eyes lit up as she took the last bite of her gyro. "Is this gonna change my life forever?" she asked as she picked up the chocolate baklava.

"It just might," I said gravely.

She grinned and took her first bite, her eyes closing as she chewed. "Oh my gosh, this is amazing." Once again, talking with a full mouth. "You were right, this is life changing."

"Isn't it?"

If only it could be this easy all the time, just me and her and our gyros and baklava. No controlling father, no rules, no curfews and sneaking around.

I hated to break the spell, but a quick glance at the clock on the wall told me it was getting quite late and while I didn't know when her father would be getting back, I knew enough to realize that she'd better be there when he did.

"We should probably head out," I said as she finished her piece of baklava.

"Probably." She licked her fingers while she eyed my piece.

"Do you want mine too?" I asked with a grin, offering it to her.

"Are you sure?" she asked, but she was already reaching for it.

"Yes, I'm sure." I laughed. "Go ahead, have at it."

While she ate the last of the baklava, I cleaned up our table, dumping the trash and putting the tray on top. She met me by the door, licking her hands clean before wiping them on a napkin and throwing it out.

"That was one of the best meals I've ever eaten," she said, sighing happily. "Thank you."

We made our way back towards the hotel, walking slowly, hand in hand.

Sarah sighed when she saw the hotel, letting go of my hand and turning to face me. "Will I see you at the wedding tomorrow?"

I nodded. "Yes, I'll be working.".

"Well, you'll get to see me all dressed up," she said shyly, reaching up and running her fingers through her hair.

"I'm looking forward to it."

She grinned. "Then I guess I'll see you tomorrow. Thank you for today, Keith."

As I watched her walk away I said, "have a good night, Phee."

I turned towards the employee parking, my thoughts running all over the place. Yes, I would see her tomorrow. But I would see her while I was working and she would be there as a guest, with probably lots of eligible young men chasing after her while I watched from the sidelines.

Could there ever be a time and place for us to be together when we were so different?

As much as I wanted to believe there could be, I wasn't sure.

Sarah

My parents were out at some charity event or something, and I was supposed to be resting before the wedding, but all I could think about was if I could manage to sneak downstairs.

Keith had said that he would be working this evening. Would he be here yet?

Without knowing exactly when my parents would be back, it was a risk, but I could say I had just gone down to get a drink from the bar if they asked.

They couldn't get that upset about that.

Well, they probably could, and would, but if I was lucky, they wouldn't ever find out.

Either way, it would be worth it if I got to spend more time with Keith.

So, I quickly grabbed my shoes and baseball cap, pulled on Keith's hoodie, and made my way downstairs, hoping that if I acted confident enough, no one would stop to talk to me or ask themselves if I was the heiress from the penthouse.

I made it to the second floor, where the ballroom was located, and it only took me a couple of minutes to find Keith. He was there, carrying some chairs into a mostly empty conference room. I snuck up behind him and reached out to tap his shoulder, laughing when he jumped. "Surprise."

"You scared me," he said, reaching out for me but pulling back before he could touch me.

"I'm sorry?" I said, though I didn't really mean it.

"You should be." The chairs had clattered to the floor and I helped him pick them up again. "What are you doing here?"

I shrugged. "I was bored."

"You probably shouldn't be down here," he said quietly.

I looked around the room to where a couple of bellhops were helping set up chairs. "I mean, unless they're gonna tattle on me, I don't see any reason why I can't be down here."

He looked over at the other two bellhops and nodded. "I can probably keep them quiet, but you can't be down here for long."

"I will leave when you tell me to," I said, crossing my heart. "Can I help with anything?"

"You're going to get me in trouble, you know that?"

The other bellhops noticed my presence and elbowed each other, whispering and staring at me. Keith groaned. "Well, now you've done it. Now they're never gonna leave me alone."

"Should I be sorry?"

"Yes, yes, you should." Keith shook his head as the braver of the two, or the one chosen to be the sacrifice, approached us.

"Hello, Miss Hanson," he said. "Can we help you with anything?"

"Miss Hanson, meet David," Keith said. "She would like to help us set up for the wedding."

The announcement must have been so unexpected that David's mouth actually dropped open. Unable to resist any longer, the other bellhop hurried over, clearly afraid of missing out on the fun.

"Hello, Miss Hanson. I'm Mark."

"Miss Hanson wants to help us set up," David said, eyes wide.

"Is there a problem with that?" I asked with what I knew was a winning smile. If they were on our side, nobody would get in trouble. "It sounds like fun."

"'Fun' isn't exactly what I would call it," one of them muttered before Keith elbowed him.

"Miss Hanson doesn't want anyone telling her father that she wanted to help. Capeesh?"

"Oh, yeah. Got it," David said quickly. "We can do that."

"Wonderful. Now, what can I help with?" I asked.

"Let her do the frilly stuff," David said, glancing at me. "How are you with ribbon?"

"I can find my way around some ribbon." I could figure it out, at least.

"All right, Miss Hanson, you're on ribbon duty." David pointed to a box by the door. "We'll finish these chairs for you. They want ribbon lining the aisle so folks don't wander into it during the ceremony. Does that make sense?"

I nodded. "Absolutely. Just make it pretty."

"Exactly," Keith said with an approving smile, picking up his pile of chairs again. While the boys carried chairs and lined them up in neat rows, I went to the box by the door and pulled out a wide satin ribbon.

"Let's line up the center aisle first so she can see what she's working with," Keith said, and a few minutes later, I had an entire aisle.

"Thank you," I said, looking up at him as he passed me with a wink.

I looped ribbon around chairs and tied knots and bows, and after maybe an hour, the aisle was laid out beautifully, if I did say so myself. The chairs were all lined up nicely, and the boys had added an arbor with draping flowers that didn't look quite right, but they'd done their best. "The florist is going to come and finish those," Keith said, appearing behind me as I tilted my head to study the arbor. "We just had to get them on there so they didn't have to start with nothing. Now we're heading to the other ballroom to set up the reception. Are you still with us, or do you need to get back?"

"I'm with you," I said, stretching my back. Kneeling for an hour wasn't something I usually did.

I followed Keith, David, and Mark into the ballroom next door, which was even larger, with round tables and a dance floor already set up, but no chairs, no decorations, not even tablecloths.

"We're going to start with chairs if you want to work on table-cloths," Keith said. "They're in those totes over there." He gestured off to the side of the room where there were several large totes. "They want ivory tablecloths, not white. I'm assuming that you'll know the difference."

I laughed. "Leave it to me."

"I was planning on it," he said, his hand brushing my arm as he walked past me towards the chair racks.

The chairs were nearly done and I only had a few tables left when a woman in black slacks and a floral print blouse walked in. "Gentlemen, would you mind helping me bring all the flowers up?" she asked.

"Of course," Keith said, setting down the last chair that he had, beckoning for Mark and David to join him. He glanced at me on his way out the door and I nodded to show that I was okay.

By the time they came back, I'd finished putting the tablecloths on and was just straightening a few of them. "How beautiful," the florist said, looking around the room. "This will do nicely."

As the bellhops came back with the cart covered in plastic storage bins, she dusted off her hands. "Now, let's get to work."

"How can I help?" I asked.

"I have bouquets to go in all of these vases, which need to be set on each of the tables on top of these mirrors with those candles." She gestured to various bins as she spoke.

"That sounds complicated," I said. "Sounds fun."

The florist laughed. "I'm glad you think so. Let me show you how I want them."

We opened the first bin and she pulled out a vase with a beautifully arranged bouquet. I walked over to another bin and pulled out a mirror, and she found three candles in another. After a moment of instruction, she had one centerpiece finished.

One down—only thirty more tables to go. "Do you think you can replicate this on some of the other tables?" she asked.

"Absolutely." There was still plenty of work to do and I still had time, so I could definitely help with at least a little of it. And if there was one thing I could do, it was make a centerpiece look good.

"Then let's get started."

Before long, the ballroom, which had appeared to be a stale conference room when I entered, was looking like a fairytale palace. Keith, David, and Mark had been busy stringing up fairy lights while we worked on the flowers. The centerpieces were beautifully arranged, and the catering company had arrived and was laying out place settings on each table. The room that had been so empty was now full, and I had been part of it, which felt amazing.

I adjusted a few flowers in one of the bouquets that seemed off compared to some of the other ones. I wasn't nervous until I looked over and noticed the florist was standing next to me, watching silently.

"You've got an eye for this," she said. "Have you ever considered becoming a florist?"

I laughed a little and shook my head. "No. As fun as that sounds, I don't think it's for me."

"Well, you're quite good at it. Let me know if that's something you're ever interested in doing." She handed me a card. "Thank you for all your help today–it was greatly appreciated. I'm going to go work on the arch in the ceremony room if you'd like to come assist me."

"Yes, I'll be there in a minute."

I had to tell Keith before I left. I didn't want him to think I'd just wandered off without saying goodbye.

I adjusted a few final things on the centerpieces as I made my way across the room to Keith, who was helping the caterer carry things in. He looked up at me and our eyes met across the room. His smile seemed to say a thousand things, none of which I understood, but all of them filled me with warmth.

I looked back down at the centerpiece I was still touching, proud of what I'd accomplished, knowing it was the first time I'd ever really done something with my own hands. I adjusted one more flower, making sure it found the perfect place in the bouquet.

Yes, this was a wonderful feeling.

"It looks beautiful," a voice said over my shoulder, and I turned to see Keith smiling proudly at me. "Good job."

"Thank you." The praise made me blush. "It's beautiful, isn't it? I didn't do much."

"Yeah, okay, don't lie, I saw you rearranging it," he said with a smirk.

"She said I did a good job too," I said sheepishly. Admitting it made me happy.

"Are you going to help her finish?"

"Yes, she's working on the arch now. I'll see you later, then?"

"I'll be in that room in a little bit, making sure it's all good before I go get ready. Hurry, though. It's getting late."

He was right. I was running out of time, but I couldn't resist being there for the final touches.

I helped the florist finish the arch, then watched her mess with the ribbons that I'd arranged in the aisle and was proud to see that she only made a few slight tweaks. Apparently I was better at this than I thought.

It was only a few minutes later, when the first guest arrived, that I realized I wasn't dressed for the wedding that was meant to start in probably twenty or thirty minutes. At least I'd already showered.

I said goodbye to the florist, who thanked me once again for my help, and hurried down the aisle towards the door. As I burst through it, I ran smack into Keith, who caught me around the waist as we both fell off-balance.

"You okay?" he asked, inspecting me.

"Sorry, yes, I'm fine, I just realized I'm not dressed."

He looked down at me and grinned. "You look dressed to me."

"Oh my gosh, stop," I said, laughing. "You know what I mean."

"I do, but it's so much fun to tease you," he admitted. "You'd better run, though." He let go of my waist and I missed his hand as soon as it was gone.

"I'll be back," I said with a smile, dashing towards the elevator. I'd better be dressed before my parents were ready to come down, or I would have some serious explaining to do.

It was worth any amount of explaining for the fun that I'd had in the past two hours, though.

I watched Sarah run for the elevator. Would she look back at me? I was rewarded with a smile as she waited for the doors to open, slipping through them quickly and pressing the button for the penthouse.

"So," a voice said behind me, and I turned to see Mark and David grinning from ear to ear.

"Oh, shut up," I said.

"You've been holding out on us," David said, pointing a finger at me.

"It's not like that."

"I don't believe a word of that," David said.

"Did you see the way she was looking at him?" Mark asked David, pointedly ignoring me.

"Would you just shut up," I said, rolling my eyes. "And don't say anything."

Laughter followed me down the hallway as I went to change into a formal waiter outfit. How long would it take Sarah to get dressed and ready for the wedding? Would she make it down in time?

Not that it mattered to me. I wouldn't get to see her until the reception, where I would be helping with the catering. But I wondered if she'd be ready in time for her parents.

The hour and a half before the reception seemed to drag on forever, and the sly looks from Mark and David didn't help. Every time I came across the two of them, they were whispering and cackling and nudging each other, giving me looks that gave me no confidence in their ability to keep their mouths shut. But what could I do? Nothing really except pray that they wouldn't say anything to anyone.

This was why I hadn't wanted anybody at work to see us together. Not that it wasn't worth it to spend that extra time with her. But they were going to be really annoying now.

As guests slowly made their way into the reception, I kept my eyes peeled for Sarah. The couple had decided to have their receiving line outside the reception door, which didn't make any sense to me, but it wasn't my wedding. It made for a very slow first couple of minutes, though.

I was carrying around a tray of appetizers when I noticed David nudging Mark and gesturing towards the door, a sure sign something was going on.

And there she was.

I almost dropped my tray. She was wearing a dark blue lace gown that hugged her every curve before flaring out at her hips in a soft fabric that begged to be touched, with enough pleats to make the dress very "spin-y" in a way that would have made my sisters green with envy when they were younger.

You weren't supposed to upstage the bride at a wedding, but Sarah eclipsed every woman here.

She looked around the room, finding Mark and David first with a slight smile and an acknowledgement that made them both turn red. So red, I could see it from across the room. She grinned at that, and then continued her survey of the room until she found me. She smiled and the whole world stopped for a moment as our eyes met. But all too soon, she had to walk away, following her parents to their table. Which was, of course, on the other side of the room from where I was working.

Mark and David were working that side of the room.

I should have looked at the damn name cards.

Mark quickly made his way over to her to ask if she needed water or anything, as we were asking each table. Her father barked at him and Mark scurried off. What had he said?

Sarah was seated facing away from me. I could see the back of her neck and not much else—it was enough to torture me, though.

I carried on with my job, serving people, filling waters, trying to focus on anything but the devastatingly perfect girl just out of reach.

"It's not working," a voice said over my shoulder, and I turned to see David. "We can tell."

"Tell what?" I asked, though I knew what he was going to say.

"You're hopelessly infatuated with her. Come on. I'll switch with you."

I couldn't hide my grin as I clapped him on the back and made my way across the room to stand by Mark.

I had the best coworkers in the world.

Mark grinned at me. "It's nothing, huh?"

"Oh, shut up."

Never mind, they weren't the best.

He laughed far louder than we were supposed to and quickly shut up as several of the guests looked at us. Leaning in, he muttered through his teeth. "Yeah, I see how that's going for you. You're not good at this."

"Shut up," I whispered again.

Jerk.

During the cocktail hour, when there was a bit more mingling happening, Sarah came up next to me and my heart nearly stopped as I looked down at her.

She was absolutely beautiful in every way.

And I couldn't say anything about it.

"Thank you," she said, accepting a miniature caprese skewer from my tray. "This looks delicious."

"It is delicious," I said with a small smile.

She was delicious.

And the look on her face told me that she knew exactly what I was thinking.

"You're right," she said, savoring the bite and licking her lips with a wicked look in her eyes. "I think I'll have another." She reached over and took another before winking at me and walking away.

I was totally screwed.

If this was my reaction to her appearing next to me, how was I gonna make it through the rest of this wedding?

I did my best to ignore her through dinner, but then the dancing started and I had to watch Sarah walk onto the dance floor with another man, and it felt like a knife to my stomach.

Why did it hurt so much? All I knew was that I wanted nothing more than to make her mine so that she would never dance with another man ever again.

Because that was totally going to happen.

I tried to mind my own business and tried to look away from her as I refilled drinks for a table of old ladies, but it was almost impossible and my heart jumped for joy when she appeared next to me a few songs later.

"Are you done serving?" she asked.

"Not quite, why?"

She shrugged. "I don't know…I was thinking maybe you'd want to dance with me."

I stared at her, my brain not quite computing the words that she'd said. "I'm working."

Sarah smiled. "I know you're working."

I looked around the room, full of young men in tuxes, all of whom would love to dance with her. "You really want me to dance?"

"That's actually about the only thing I want right now." Her eyes twinkled as she looked up at me. "Are you going to tell me no?"

"We shouldn't," I warned quietly, but everything in me wanted to dance with her. To wrap my arms around her and show everyone that she had chosen me.

Even if she couldn't really choose me.

"What about your dad?" I asked.

"He stepped out to take a phone call. It's up to you," she said. But her voice trembled a little, and I knew that asking had been difficult for her. The last thing she wanted was for me to turn her down.

With as much as I wanted to dance with her, I couldn't say no.

"You are dangerous, you know that?" I asked, setting my tray on a side table, allowing her to take my hand and lead me to the dance floor.

Mark and David watched from across the room, grinning like fools, as Sarah pulled me into a waltz form.

Suddenly, I was thankful for the times our childhood friend Jeremiah, who was now a Broadway dancer, had taught my brother and I how to waltz with our sisters. It meant that I wouldn't make a fool of myself in front of my heiress.

Sarah smiled up at me as I began to lead her around the floor. "You know how to dance." She sounded a little surprised.

"I do. My mother insisted that we learn." I could leave out the part about a boy two years younger than me teaching me.

"I wasn't sure if you would know how," she admitted.

"And yet you pulled me out for a waltz anyway."

"I wanted to waltz with you. Especially after that last dance."

"What happened?" I asked, every instinct in me threatening to kill whoever had hurt her.

"Nothing, really," she said quickly. "He just wasn't you."

"I suppose that's an acceptable reason." I spun her into a dip, then back up again.

"You're pretty good at this," she said, her cheeks flushed.

"My mother also insisted on lots of practice."

She laughed as I spun her around, wishing we could live in this moment for a lifetime. Beautiful music and a beautiful girl–what more could any man want?

And then reality came crashing in.

"Sarah Hanson," a man yelled and time stopped, Sarah's eyes widening in terror. The band crashed to a discordant halt along with us, triggering everyone else on the dance floor to stop and stare.

"Oh no," Sarah said, her voice trembling. "I'm so sorry, Keith." She looked over my shoulder, her breathing growing faster, and I turned to see who was coming, to put myself between her and whoever had scared her.

It was her father.

The one person who I was powerless against.

His face was nearly purple with anger as he closed the distance between us rapidly.

"You come with me," he said, reaching past me to grab Sarah's arm, pulling her off the dance floor.

Sarah looked up at me, her face frozen in fear as she followed her father.

I followed her, wishing I dared to demand that he release her.

Mr. Hanson dragged Sarah through the wedding reception and out into the hallway. "How dare you dance with a server?" he demanded, releasing her. She took a step backwards into me, my hand coming to rest on the small of her back where her father couldn't see. "You're hurting our reputation."

"I don't care about our reputation," she said. "For once in my life, I was enjoying myself, and then you interrupted, which was far more damaging to our reputation than anything I did."

"You were enjoying yourself with an employee?" her father asked, his face turning darker. I'd never seen a man change so many shades.

"Keith is more than an employee, he's my friend." Sarah was still trembling, but her voice was strong. "He's been my friend since we first started coming here, and I don't regret asking him to dance with me."

Mr. Hanson turned to me. "So you're fraternizing with the patrons, then? That's grounds for being fired." The color in his face dissipated as he drew himself up to his full height. "I'll see you ruined for this."

"He didn't do anything wrong," Sarah said desperately. "It's not his fault."

"He knew better," Mr. Hanson thundered. "As one of our employees, he knew better than to talk to you, and he did it anyway."

"Dad, I was the one who wouldn't stop talking to him. None of this is his fault."

"Well, you knew better too," her father said.

"Dad, no, stop."

"Clearly this has gone on long enough." He stared at me, a dark stare that left no room for arguments or talking back. "You are fired."

"No," Sarah gasped.

His gaze moved to her. "Another word out of you, Sarah, and you will regret it. Upstairs, now. And you, whatever your name is? Get out of my hotel. You'll never work in another hotel, not if I have anything to do with it."

Sarah shrank into my touch and I swallowed hard, knowing there was nothing I could do to help her now. She tried to take my hand, which only enraged her father more.

He lunged forward and pulled her away from me, and Sarah burst into tears, looking back at me before yanking her hand away from her father and running for the grand staircase.

Mr. Hanson stared me down as I made my way towards the staff door.

There was nothing that would change his mind. I had broken the rules. I had become friends—or maybe more—with a hotel patron.

I knew what I was doing was wrong, and I did it anyway.

My future had just been completely changed.

How did it all go so wrong?

Sarah

How could such a wonderful evening have turned awful so quickly?

I rushed down the hallway, knowing my father was following me. I wanted to get into my room and lock the door so I wouldn't have to listen to him, because he was not happy and I didn't want to hear it.

I fumbled for my room key in the hidden pocket of my skirt and opened the door, closing it as quickly as I could before rushing into my bedroom and locking the door behind me. I slid to the floor in tears.

A few moments later, my father banged on my bedroom door. "We need to talk, Sarah."

How had everything turned upside down so quickly? Where could we go from here?

It was probably better if I never saw Keith again.

Maybe if I ignored Keith, my father wouldn't follow through on his threat of blacklisting him, although he seemed angry enough to do it right now.

"Sarah, let me in," my father demanded.

I walked into my en suite bathroom and closed the door, turning on the shower to drown out the sounds of my father.

I didn't want to listen to him right now. There was nothing he could say that I wanted to hear unless it was, *I'm sorry, I've changed my mind, I love you, I accept you,* or any variations of the above.

But I knew well enough to realize that would never happen.

Tears ran down my face as I sat down on the bathroom floor, pulling my knees to my chest as much as the dress would let me.

The night had been so absolutely wonderful until the moment when my father came back from an unusually short phone call and saw me dancing with one of his employees.

It had been a beautiful wedding. I'd been a part of creating something so incredible and it had been so fulfilling. And the sight of Keith in a suit had made my heart race.

He looked absolutely amazing in a suit.

Now I probably wouldn't ever get to see him again, because I had dared to dream that something might change and that my happiness was worth it.

How could I have been so foolish?

I should have known better. I should have known that my father would never dare to let me have happiness. I should have known that dancing with Keith would only enrage him and bring about the future that Keith had been warning me about since we first started talking. The future that I knew was all too real of a possibility.

I should have known better.

And how could I make this up to Keith? If he even wanted to see me again.

Would he even want to talk to me?

He'd understood this could happen. I'd understood this could happen. But I'd been the one stupid enough to push the limit.

How could I make up for him losing his job because of me?

I should have seen that nothing could happen between us, even if he did make me happy. I should have realized that Keith was too wonderful for someone like me. There was no way that we were meant to be together. We lived in separate worlds and I should have known better than to try to mix them. I was foolish, blinded by the idea of someone who saw me for me. A society marriage was my role in life and I should have known better than to try for anything else.

Such a stupid, foolish girl.

My phone vibrated in my pocket and I almost didn't look at it.

It was probably just Dad.

But what if it was Keith?

The thought was almost paralyzing. With indecision raging, I pulled out my phone and stared at the dark screen for almost a minute before I got up to the nerve to tap on it.

It was him.

Call me when you can.

Somehow I knew that he was more worried for me than I was for him, so I called him immediately.

"Are you okay?" he asked without any hesitation.

"I'm fine," I reassured him.

"Are you sure?"

"I'm sure." I could hear the tenseness in his voice.

"He didn't hurt you?"

"He would never hurt me," I said automatically. "What about you, are you okay?"

"I'm fine," he said.

"I don't know that I believe you."

He gave a little chuckle. "I promise. I'm fine. A little sad, maybe, but I know I'll be fine. I'm more worried about you."

"I'm okay," I said again. He still didn't seem sure of it, but I didn't know that I'd be able to convince him without letting him see me for himself, and that clearly wasn't going to happen. I was going to be on room arrest until we left for home.

"So how do we fix this?" he asked.

There was a lump in my throat as I thought about his question. Typical man, trying to fix things. But what was there to fix?

"I don't know that we can," I said after a moment.

The silence on the other side of the phone was deafening. "You can't mean that."

My heart hurt, having to say the words. "Really, I don't know that we can fix this, Keith. As much as I wish we could, we're from different worlds."

"If there's one thing I know from watching my parents, who've been married for almost thirty years, it's that you can always fix things," he said, with a fire in his words that told me he would never stop trying to make things work between us. "I'm not giving up."

But what could we do?

"I think we need to." My heart broke as I said it. "I think it's time to give up."

"You don't really believe that, do you?" he asked softly. "You really want to give up on us? Or is this just your father in your head?"

There was a lump in my throat bigger than the state of California. Did I really believe it? I wasn't one hundred percent sure that I did. But I knew that Keith would never give up unless I convinced him to. It was the only way he would stop fighting for me.

What choice did I have? He would never be accepted into my life or my family. I knew firsthand how difficult my world was when you were part of it–but when you weren't? I couldn't do that to him.

"It's not just my father," I choked out.

He deserved more than to be shunned by my family and forced out of his chosen career.

He deserved a girl who could give him everything he'd ever wanted. A different family who would adore him and who wouldn't stand in the way of him and his dreams.

He deserved more than me; he deserved more than someone who would actively destroy him.

"If you truly believe that, if it's not your father talking," he said, his voice cracking, "then I guess there's nothing else to say. Goodbye, Phee. Good luck with your life."

There was a beep as he hung up. I looked down at my phone as his picture disappeared and burst into tears.

I didn't stop crying for the rest of the night.

All I wanted was to feel his arms around me and wake up to find out that this was all a bad dream.

But I knew that it wasn't and it was all my fault.

January

With no job and nothing else to do, I'd spent the past couple weeks...okay, more like a month...in my room, studying.

I knew everyone was worried about me. I could hear them whispering in the hallway and I could see the looks that they shot me when they thought I wasn't looking.

But I was fine. Right? I could live without my job and the girl who I'd accidentally fallen head over heels for.

I would be fine.

Clearly, nobody else thought so. They spent the vast majority of their time tiptoeing around me like I would break if anyone so much as mentioned the word "work," or a job, or anything else.

"It's not like it would have worked anyway," I overheard Natalie whispering to Kait in the hallway. "I don't think it's possible for a relationship to work out when money is involved like that."

Kait sighed. "I know, believe me, especially after my last disaster. I wish they had worked out, though. She was just so perfect for him, and she fit in with the family so well."

Not that we were all comparing Sarah to Ashley, but Ashley came up severely wanting. Every time she came over now, the family was frosty with her, and it was impossible to not remember that night.

"I just don't know how long he'll be hurting like this. I hope it's not very long," Kait said.

As much as I tried to put on a brave face for my family, life sucked right now. And obviously they had absolutely no idea I could hear them in the hallway, because if they did, they wouldn't be saying the things they were. But hearing them talk only reminded me how miserable I was and how much everything hurt.

So, thanks for that, Kaitlyn.

I put down my notebook and pencil and stretched out my legs, leaning back in my swivel chair and staring up at the ceiling. My last exam had happened and my college career was over.

My hotel career might be over, too, and the hospitality degree that I'd spent four years working on would be wasted.

There had to be some hotel out there that wasn't under Hanson's control, right?

It might be a motel instead of the hotels I'd dreamed of managing, but it would be a job in my field.

I sighed. If only things had gone differently.

Kait kept telling me that I shouldn't wonder what things could have been like, that the wondering and pining would be the end of me. She'd tried bonding with me over the pain of recent breakups but, as much as I appreciated her trying, it was different. It wasn't like her ex's dad had destroyed their relationship.

Though Sarah had been the one to tell me that we were over, so maybe it wasn't just her dad.

Still, I couldn't help wishing he would change his mind.

Like that would ever happen.

But if he would... well, maybe she would change her mind too. Because I missed her. I missed her constantly. Every time my phone made a noise, I rushed to see if it was her, even though I knew that it wouldn't be. Every time there was a knock at the front door, I wondered if somehow she'd gotten away and come to see me. And every time it was just a delivery, my heart broke all over again.

The pain had to stop sometime, right? I wouldn't miss her for the rest of my life. I would find a way to move on eventually.

But for now, it just hurt like hell.

I was wearing the sweatshirt that Sarah had borrowed after our torrential downpour hike, and it still smelled like her. Yes, I was a whole new level of pathetic, but I couldn't make myself care. Was it healthy to be wearing it? Probably not. Did I care? No.

There was a knock on my door and Mom let herself in when I called, "Come in."

She sat down on my bed and waited for me to turn in my swivel chair to face her. I did so slowly, knowing this was going to be another heart-to-heart moment that I didn't really want to have.

"How are you doing?" she asked.

I snorted. I tried not to, I really did, but I couldn't help it. "How do you think it's going, Mom?" But then I sighed. Mom wasn't the reason I was upset, and it wasn't fair to take my sarcasm out on her. "It's not going great."

"I know." She smiled a sad smile. "You've been trying so hard, but I could tell. I'm your mother, after all."

"And a very observant one, at that."

Mom smiled. "Well, it is my job."

She waited a couple of moments to see if I would say anything before she leaned closer, resting her elbows on her knees. "So you're just going to give her up."

"I don't have any other option," I said. "Her father would never let anything happen."

"So you're going to let her go gracefully and move on with your life and pretend nothing ever happened between you."

Well shit, that didn't sound appealing.

Mom laughed at the look on my face. "Yeah, I know, it didn't sound good to me either. Keith, my dear, one thing that I have tried to teach all of my children is how important it is to never give up on the people you care about. Because life isn't easy and, no matter how perfect you think someone is, there isn't one person who will be the perfect magical fit in your life, who will fill all your needs and not give you any heartache in return. You have to fight through the hard times to get to the wonderful times. I don't know that you've given it everything with Sarah, and I would hate for you to regret that for the rest of your life."

"I tried," I said, "but in this case, I don't think it's meant to be."

Mom laughed again. "Why do you get to decide what's meant to be? That's up to God, not you."

"But what do you do if they've decided that you're not worth it?" I asked bitterly, the words coating my tongue with an awful aftertaste.

"Do you know that she doesn't think you're worth it? Or do you think she was parroting something that her father has told her so many times that she now believes it herself? Or maybe it was even something he told her to say."

"Believe me, the thought has crossed my mind more than once that her father was telling her to say it. But she said it without any hesitation. She didn't think that we had something worth fighting for. She thought it would be better for us to let it go. How can I argue with that?"

Mom let me sit in silence for a moment before saying, "I know you want to fight for her, and I know you're having a hard time deciding if it's worth it or not. But I will tell you this, my boy. It is always worth fighting for someone you love. Because even if you aren't the right person for her, I think your Sarah might need someone to show her that she's worth fighting for. And if that someone is you? Well, you never know what could happen."

Her words made my heart beat faster.

She was right.

Sarah did need someone to show her that she was worth fighting for.

She'd spent her whole life under her father's thumb and no one had ever made the effort to show her that she deserved more than that.

But it wasn't going to be easy.

"I don't know that there's anything I can do, though. I'm pretty sure she blocked my phone number and I don't know where she lives."

"That's what Google is for."

"She's an heiress, Mom. She's not going to have her address listed on Google Maps."

Mom shrugged. "Well, if there's no way then there's no way. I guess you'll just have to give up on her." She smiled innocently, but she knew exactly what she was doing.

We were Palmers. We didn't back down from a challenge.

And those words were definitely a challenge.

Every part of me wanted to instantly respond that of course I wasn't giving up. She'd pretty much guaranteed that I wouldn't let Sarah go without a fight.

Thanks a lot, Mom.

"You suck," I said, leaning over and kissing her cheek.

"I know." She smiled sweetly and stood to walk out of my room. "I love you, dear," she said before she closed the door.

I reached over and pulled out my laptop.

It was time to find an heiress who didn't want to be found.

Sarah

My finger paused over my phone as I stared down at a picture and a lump caught in my throat. Yes, I was being that lame person who scrolled through all of the social media apps to try to find a glimpse of their ex, and I couldn't stop.

Keith didn't have any social media himself other than an Instagram page that he had never posted on. But his sisters, especially Krystal, posted frequently, and he was in several of their photos.

So here I was, reduced to the position of miserable social scroller, wishing that I could be seeing him in person and not just through my far too small screen.

There was only one recent photo since we'd said goodbye. A selfie of Krystal at game night with the family, including Keith, in the background.

He looked tired.

Was he as miserable as I was, or was it an act?

Not that he had any reason for it to be an act, but somehow it partially made me feel better if I thought he was fine with it.

Why, I wasn't sure. It shouldn't have made me feel better to know that he was miserable. And yet somehow, it did.

I tossed my phone next to me and rolled over on the bed, burying my face in my pillow. I should have known better than to fall for his stupid face, stupid smile, stupid amazing family.

Stupid me.

It was all my fault. I'd set myself up for failure. And yet I couldn't bring myself to regret any moment that I'd spent with Keith and the Palmers. If anything, thinking about them just made me miss them more.

There was a knock on my door and I sighed. It had to be Mom. She was the only one who would bother me in my room. "Come in," I called, not bothering to look up from my pillow.

Mom walked in and sat next to me on my bed. I didn't have to look at her to know that she was sitting on the edge, feet crossed at the ankles, hands folded firmly in her lap. Ever the perfect society wife, even in her daughter's bedroom.

"You didn't come down for breakfast," Mom said.

"I wasn't hungry this morning."

Mom waited half a beat before asking cautiously, "Are you okay?"

I let out a sarcastic chuckle. Only my mom would witness me getting my heart broken and then wait several weeks to ask if I was okay. "I'm fine, Mom."

"You keep saying that, but you're not acting like yourself," Mom said.

I looked up at her in surprise, rolling over. "What do you mean, I'm not acting like myself?"

"You're not being yourself," Mom said with a slight shoulder shrug, so out of character for herself, "and it makes me sad. I miss my happy Sarah."

Mom had actually noticed a difference?

"I miss her too," I said softly.

Mom hesitated. "You know, darling, if this isn't the life you want, you are free to make your own choices, despite everything your father says."

I scoffed and sat up, pulling my knees into my chest. "Like that's true. He would disown me before I could get five feet out of the door. And what would I do then? I don't have any useful skills. I thought about it, you know? Even if I left, even if I said a giant 'eff you' to Dad and all of his rules, where would I go? My whole life has prepared me to be a society wife and not much more. I have nothing."

"That's not quite true," Mom said. "You still have your bank account."

"You know Dad would freeze that before I could even think about making a withdrawal. Honestly, he probably already has."

"No, your account that he doesn't know about."

"I don't know how much I would need to survive. Do you think it would even be enough?"

Mom shrugged. "I don't know how much you have in there, but it's probably enough to at least get started. And I have some tucked away, too. If you don't enjoy this life, then I don't want you stuck here. I've been part of this world long enough to know that if you hate it, the last thing I want is for you to be trapped in it." She looked so sad, and I wondered how much I didn't know about my mother. "Look, what I'm trying to say, Sarah, is that if you want to find a way to be with Keith, I will support you."

Tears filled my eyes without my permission. "I don't think he wants me anymore," I said. "I hurt him."

"That's what real love is," Mom said softly. "You hurt the people you love sometimes. The other part of love is loving them enough to fight, to win them back."

Should I be taking relationship advice from my mother, who was trapped in a loveless marriage? On the other hand, maybe she had a different perspective than everyone else.

"I saw the two of you. That boy loves you."

"Well, he did then," I said.

Mom shook her head. "That kind of love doesn't disappear just because circumstances get in the way."

I thought back to the miserable photo I'd seen earlier. He didn't seem like he'd forgotten me.

"The two of you have something special," Mom said. "I think it's time for you to realize that and start fighting for it. I know your father made a hash of things, and I'm sorry about that. If I could, well...." She trailed off, visibly fighting for control. Who knew it would take me losing Keith to see an emotional side to my mother?

"I know you would, Mom. I know."

Mom wrestled her emotions down and continued, "You have more power than you know, my Seraphina. Even if your father is upset at you. You are smart and talented, and you have money. That is more than a lot of people can say. There isn't much that you can't do. I made that secret account for you for a reason. That money is there for you to do whatever you want with it, and if what you want is to run away from your father and be with that boy, then that's what I want you to do with it. Because you deserve to be happy."

There was a lump in my throat as I leaned over and hugged my mother. "Thank you," I whispered as I held her tight for a moment.

There were tears in her eyes as she pulled away. "Even without your father's support, you are still a Hanson. You can do a lot for that boy's career, even if your father doesn't approve, just because of your last name. I know it may seem like you're stuck, but believe me, darling, you have more options than you know. And I will love you always, no matter what."

She was right.

I did have more options than I knew.

I was in charge of my own future, and that future did not involve marrying some boy who just wanted me for my name. That future involved fighting for the boy who loved me for me, even if I'd ruined things.

"Thanks, Mom," I said, swallowing the lump in my throat. "I love you."

"I love you too. Now, go get your boy."

For the first time in many days, I smiled. "That sounds like a plan to me."

I reached underneath my bed and pulled out the luggage that I kept underneath, and Mom got up with a smile. "I guess I'll call the plane for you," she said. "I can get you there before your father realizes what's going on and tries to cut you off."

"I can take it from there," I said.

And for the first time, I felt like I actually could.

I was my own person, with my own future, and I deserved to be happy. And if that meant I had to chase down happiness and fight for it, then that's what I would do.

Keith

I stood in the airport security line, clutching the ticket that I'd bought with the last of my money. It was time for the grandest gesture of my life and I had no idea how it was gonna play out. But I had to try. I would be forever upset at myself if I didn't try.

So, here I was at the airport, barely sure if I had her address right or if she would even let me see her when I got there.

All I had was a small carry-on, my hopes and dreams, and faith that we were worth it.

I looked over to the line of people on their way out of the airport. There were families there waiting for reunion, grandmothers greeting grandchildren, a young woman throwing her arms around a soldier.

What would Sarah's reaction be when she saw me? Would it be a happy reunion? Would she slap me for daring to track her down? Would she burst into tears? Would I?

Someone ran through the line, dodging around people in her rush.

She looked just like my Sarah, but there was no way it was her. Sarah was in California. The odds of both of us being at the airport at the same time had to be basically zero. Right?

She just looked like her. There was no way it was really her.

But then the girl stopped to read the sign pointing out which way to exit and my heart skipped a beat. Because when she stopped moving, it was extremely obvious that she was my Sarah.

How?

I pushed my way out of the security line and shouted, "Seraphina."

She turned, wildly looking everywhere until she saw me, her mouth dropping open as I pushed my way towards her, my shoes in my hand, my carry-on bag bumping everyone, and my heart in my throat.

She had the most beautiful smile as she ran to me, the two of us meeting in the middle in a tangle of bags and arms and two hearts beating as one. I dropped my things and grabbed her, picking her up and spinning her around, holding her tight.

I would never let her go again.

"What are you doing here?" we asked in unison, laughing at each other as I set her back on her feet, refusing to let go of her.

"Ladies first," I said, rubbing my hand down her bare arm, feeling goosebumps rise.

"I had to see you," she said. "I don't know if you want to see me too, or if you never want to see me again, but—"

"I want to see you," I interrupted, resting my forehead against hers. "You have no idea how much I've wanted to see you."

Sarah smiled. "Really?"

"As long as you didn't come back to see Julian," I said, a smirk on my face.

Sarah shivered involuntarily. "No, please God no, never again."

I laughed, but then I got serious. "What happened to being from two different worlds?" Because if she still believed that, it didn't matter that she was here now.

"I changed my mind. The only place I want to be is in your world. It's just so much better than mine. As long as you don't mind that I'm no longer an heiress."

"Just because I fell for the heiress doesn't mean the heiress part is what I fell for. Besides, my world has been miserable without you," I admitted, pressing my lips to her temple for a quick kiss. "Does your father know you're here?"

Sarah grimaced and let out an awkward chuckle. "No, and I don't know how long Mom will be able to keep it from him." As if on cue, her phone started ringing. Sarah shook her head, reached into her pocket, and shut it off. "But I'm not dealing with him. I'm too happy to let him ruin this moment."

"Thank God," I said as her arm stole around my neck again. "Although I will say it's rather inconvenient that I spent the last of my money on a plane ticket and didn't even get to use it for a grand gesture."

Sarah laughed. "I can reimburse you for the plane ticket, if necessary. But I'm glad I beat you here, because I'm going to need someone to show me how to live a normal life, and it's awfully hard to do that in California. I'd much rather do it here with your family."

"That's definitely something I can help with."

Her eyes twinkled. "And I may not be destitute, but I'll need some help learning how to live like a normal person and not an heiress. My father has probably frozen all of my bank accounts, except for the secret one."

"I think we can work something out," I said, pulling her even closer, my arm tight around her waist as she clung to my neck.

"I look forward to it."

"You know something?" I asked.

"Hmm?"

"This is the part where I would kiss you if I weren't such a gentleman."

Sarah grinned. "You know, you're the only person I have ever wanted to break my own rules for."

"Well, if my mother hadn't taught me to always respect a woman's boundaries, I would be totally down for helping you break your rules."

"Does your mom know you're here?"

"Oh yes," I said. "Without her, I would probably still be wallowing in my room, thinking about how much I miss you and how much my sweatshirt still smells like you."

Sarah let go of me and reached into her bag with a laugh, pulling out my college sweatshirt. "I wore this constantly and it barely smells like you anymore, which I'm going to need you to fix right away, okay?"

"I'll give you an entire bottle of my cologne if you want it," I said.

"That sounds like a plan." She dropped the sweatshirt back into her bag, resting her hands on my chest as I wrapped my arms around her again.

I could hold her like this for the rest of my life.

She looked up at me with her beautiful brown eyes and asked, "Do you know something?"

"What?"

"I'm sorry for telling you that we were from different worlds and that I didn't think we belonged together. Because I don't really believe that. I love you, Keith Palmer, and I'm willing to do whatever it takes to convince you of that and how perfect we are together. I want to be part of your world and part of your family and never leave you again."

I was grinning like a fool and I couldn't stop myself. "I love you, Seraphina Hanson. I'm sorry for letting you walk away, and I'm sorry for not coming for you sooner, and I can't wait to keep you here for as long as you want to be with me."

Sarah's smile was big enough to light up the whole airport. "You mean it?"

"Forever and always," I said.

She threw her arms around me and rested her head on my chest. I held her tight, pressing a kiss to her hair, soaking in the moment. People dodged around us and they called for someone over the loudspeaker, but the general chaos of an airport was the last thing I was thinking about.

She was here. She was mine.

"I can't believe this is real," she whispered. "Are you sure this isn't a dream?"

I lightly pinched her arm and she laughed. "Nope, it's real. And if that isn't enough to convince you, the broken rib that Krystal will give you when she hugs you might be painful enough."

Sarah let go of me, reaching down to grab her bag. "Come on, let's go find your family. I want that hug. I've been dreaming about it for weeks."

"You've been dreaming about my little sister?"

She giggled. Had I ever heard her giggle before? It was adorable. "I've been dreaming about your entire family, but mostly you. Is that allowed?"

"As long as I'm in the starring role, I suppose I'll allow it," I said, leaning down to pick up my shoes and sliding them on. "Now, let's get out of here."

I couldn't wait to bring her home.

Sarah

Keith held my hand as we walked down the path to his front door and my heart was about to explode out of my chest from pure happiness.

This is what normal people felt like.

I couldn't believe that I was here with Keith, away from my father, ready to start a whole new life. Could it get any better than this?

Keith opened the front door and called for his mom, squeezing my hand.

"Maybe she's not home," I said when she didn't appear for a moment, but then his mom popped around the corner, a worried expression on her face.

"Why are you back?" she began before she saw me and her mouth dropped open. "Oh my goodness. Hello, dear." She hurried over and wrapped her arms around me in a big hug, and it took everything in me to not burst into tears.

"I'm afraid I ruined your son's grand gesture," I said, my voice cracking a little. "I hope you don't mind me arriving out of the blue."

"Not at all," she exclaimed. "Like we told you before, you are always welcome. You just had me worried. I didn't expect you to be back anytime soon."

"Yes, well, this one had other plans," Keith said, squeezing my hand and smiling at me. "She just had to beat me."

"Well, you had to wait for a commercial flight," I said. "I have a private jet, which makes it a little faster."

His mom laughed before she realized I was being serious. "Oh, well, you're right, I guess that does make things easier. What's your plan, dear?"

"I don't have one," I admitted. "I hadn't thought beyond finding Keith and telling him that I loved him."

Mrs. Palmer smiled. "Well, why don't we drop your bag in Kyle's room then, and the two of you can decide what she wants to do."

"Oh, I couldn't," I began, but she shook her head.

"Nonsense. Kyle's moved out, so he doesn't need it, and what kind of a hostess would I be if I sent you to a hotel? A very poor one."

"And if there's one thing my mother is not, it's a poor hostess," Keith said, winking at me.

"My ancestors would never forgive me," his mom said with a smile. "Besides, you need a place to crash while you figure out what you want to do, and I'm sure you both have a lot to discuss about that. Have you thought about it at all?"

"While I was on the flight, I thought a little about maybe seeing if I could do something with flowers. I really enjoyed working with the flowers at that wedding."

Keith perked up. "You would be so good at that, and I happen to know someone who might be able to help." He turned to look at his mom. "Do you think Diane is looking for a new employee?"

Mrs. Palmer shrugged. "I don't know, but I bet if you asked, she would take Sarah under her wing for at least a little bit."

Keith turned to me, his eyes sparkling. "My mom's friend Diane owns the flower shop here in town. Maybe she needs an assistant. It could be great for you. Come on, let's put your stuff in Kyle's room and we'll go talk to her."

He leaned over and picked up my bags, which we'd dropped on the floor as we greeted his mother. I followed him into his brother's old bedroom and was surprised to find a beautifully open and airy guest room, not the teenage boy haven I'd been expecting.

"I didn't even ask if you want to find something to do," Keith said while I was looking around the room. "We can wait a while, if you want some time to figure things out. Sorry, I got excited and didn't ask. I just jumped ahead."

I reached for his hand and pulled him to sit on the bed with me. "You're fine. I didn't plan on searching for a job today, but my bank account without Dad's name on it will only last for so long, and I'm sure he's already cut off my other ones since I ignored his phone call."

Though I'd made an additional five-thousand-dollar transfer into it right before I left.

How long would that last, though?

I had no idea.

Keith reached over and put an arm around my shoulders, pulling me close. "I'm so glad you're here," he said softly against my hair. "You have no idea how miserable I've been these past few weeks."

I laughed. "Probably just as miserable as I've been. My mother actually noticed that something was wrong with me."

"Well, you should have seen my sisters," Keith said. "They probably wanted to kill me."

"I'm sorry," I said with a sigh. "I caused so much hurt for all of us."

Keith shook his head. "It's okay. I might not have liked it, but we all understood why you pushed me away. Don't beat yourself up–it's in the past."

"So you don't hate me?" I asked softly.

"I will never hate you, Seraphina Hanson," he said, cupping my cheek with his free hand and tilting my face to look up at him.

"Promise?"

He kissed my forehead. "I promise. Now, come on, let's go before my siblings get home from wherever they are and we get interrupted again. I want to see if Diane needs help or if we should start putting out other feelers."

He pulled me to my feet and I took his hand, laughing as we ran through the house and out the front door, calling that we would be back as he slammed it shut behind us. He opened the car door for me like a true gentleman, handing me my seatbelt before closing it behind me.

I buckled myself into the front seat with a sigh of satisfaction, looking over at him with a smile as we drove off.

Even if I didn't find work right away, or something else to do, everything would be okay. We would get through this and everything would only get better.

He loved me.

And I loved him.

Was this real life? Was this actually happening to me? Was I really sitting in the front seat of a car with a handsome man who loved me for me, whose family loved me, who wanted me to live my life the way I wanted to live it?

How had I come so far in such a short time?

"What are you thinking about?" Keith asked, resting his hand in the middle of the console, allowing me to reach over and take it.

"Just how handsome you are," I said with a smile.

Keith blushed. "Stop teasing me."

"I'm telling the truth, but if you want to believe that I'm teasing you, that's fine." I grinned.

He rolled his eyes and kept driving, and soon we were in the town square. "Here we are," Keith said a moment later, pulling to a stop outside a flower shop. "She's right next to Mom's store." He looked over at Chickadee Lane with a smile. "She and Mom have been friends forever. I think without her, Mom never would have started Chickadee Lane. Even if she doesn't need any help, she's going to love meeting you, so don't get overwhelmed if she's super excited, okay?"

"Okay," I said with a smile. "I can't wait to meet her."

He took a deep breath, turned off the car, and ran around to open my door for me. I let him help me out and stared up at the sign over the door with hope in my heart as Keith took my hand

and led me into the store. A bell rang overhead as we walked in and a voice called out from the back, "I'll be out in one second."

"That's Diane," Keith said.

My stomach erupted in a ball of nerves as I wondered if Diane would like me.

A moment later, an attractive woman in her early fifties, maybe, stepped through the back door and stood behind the counter. "Why, it's my Keith," she said warmly, coming around to give him a hug. "Oh my goodness. You're so big."

"Yeah, I've heard that before," he said, returning the hug with an easy grin. "Diane, this is my girlfriend Sarah."

"Hello, dear," Diane said, leaning over to give me a hug of my own. I'd gotten more hugs since meeting the Palmers than I had my entire life. I didn't hate it.

"I was wondering if you were looking for an assistant," Keith said. "Sarah is new in town and she loves working with flowers. I think she does a pretty good job with them, too."

"Hmm." Diane thought about it for a minute, looking around her store. "I can't afford full-time right now," she said, "but if you wanted to come in part-time, I would be able to put you to work. Maybe not working with flowers all the time right away, but I'd be willing to train you. Unless you've already had training?"

"No," I said, "entirely self-taught."

"Why don't you put together a bouquet for me while Keith and I catch up," she said, "and we'll see what you can do?"

Nerves fluttered through my stomach, but I nodded and followed as she led the way to a table with every tool you could need. "The fridge is through here," Diane said, gesturing to a swinging door, and I walked through into a room absolutely overflowing with flowers.

It was like stepping into heaven.

Diane smiled at me. "Anyone who has that look clearly belongs here. I'll leave you to it. Take anything you want and make a beautiful arrangement for me."

With so many choices, it took me a few minutes to decide what I wanted to do and which flowers to use, but I filled my arms and walked back out to the prep counter. As Keith and Diane wandered the store talking, I trimmed the stems and pulled leaves off and started arranging in a beautiful, tall vase.

I was so happy, I felt like I could burst.

And then someone walked in, pointed at what I was making, and said that they wanted it.

I couldn't hide the grin on my face as Diane nodded approvingly. "It's a beautiful bouquet, isn't it?" she asked the customer. "As soon as she's done, I'll figure out a total for you."

She continued chatting with the customer as Keith gave me the biggest grin. I returned it before bringing my focus back to my arrangement. Now there was pressure, and I had to make it perfect.

A couple of minutes later I was done, or as close as I could be without continuing to nitpick forever. Diane rang up the customer and as they walked away with my arrangement, I didn't know if it was possible to be any happier.

"That was beautiful," Diane said, turning to me. "When can you start?"

I grinned and looked at Keith to confirm as I said, "Tomorrow, I guess?"

Diane nodded. "I'll see you then."

Keith threw his arm around my shoulders as I came around the counter. "Thanks, Diane," he said. "I'll tell Mom you said hi."

"Does this mean I'll see more of you, too?" she asked him, looking between the two of us.

"We'll see," he said, his eyes twinkling. "See you later."

He walked me out of the shop then opened my car door, and I slid into the seat with a huge grin. "I have a job," I said.

I had a job, I had a place to stay, and I had a boyfriend.

I'd ignored my dad, my mom stood up for me, and there were people here who cared about me.

I was happy.

Keith turned on the radio, which was set to the country music station, and reached over to hold my hand as we drove home together. And for the first time in my life, I felt like my future was something I could look forward to, something I could be proud of—something that I was in control of.

And that meant everything.

I was free.

One Year Later

Epilogue

KAITLYN PALMER

As a wedding photographer, I'd seen more than my fair share of starry-eyed brides, teary grooms, and passionate kisses. And yet, watching my brother kiss his bride for the first time was such a heartwarming moment, it might have beaten the *Princess Bride* kiss as the most magical of all time.

So my brother had much better luck in mixing work and personal relationships than I did.

I watched from my position in the bridal party as Keith and Sarah ran down the aisle, my smile so wide it almost hurt. Sarah's mom sat in the front row, smiling with tears running down her face. My parents sat next to her for support, instead of on the other side of the aisle. Not inviting her father had been difficult for both Sarah and her mom, but after the shit he'd said when Keith and Sarah had gotten engaged, it was probably for the best.

My studio partner Andie snapped a photo as I ran down the aisle with my brother Kyle, winking at me as I passed her. She knew how hard it was for me to be on this side of the camera and how I'd rather be with her. It showed how much I loved my brother, to be in the wedding instead of working it.

Sitting at the head table with my family had me itching to pull out my camera, and I wished that I'd snuck my backup in. Knowing that I would try to take pictures, Andie had confiscated my main camera, insisting that she was more than capable of documenting my brother's wedding and that I needed to take the night off and enjoy it. But there were so many cute moments that I was *right here* for.

Gosh, I needed to sneak up to the head table where the bride and groom couldn't see me more often.

Keith had his head bent, whispering something in Sarah's ear, while she blushed adorably. I brought my fingers up to make a fake viewfinder and composed the perfect shot, bummed that they would miss out on this.

Wait, I had my phone.

It was better than nothing.

I pulled it out of the concealed pocket in my blush-colored bridesmaid dress and snapped the shot. If it turned out well enough, I'd bully Andie into including it in their gallery.

I slipped my phone back into my pocket and looked up to find her glaring at me from across the table.

Whoops.

"Hey, friend," I said with a grin. "Can I help you?"

"Yes," she said. "Go enjoy the wedding. Go ask your father to dance with you or something."

"Nobody's dancing yet," I protested.

"We're about to start," Keith said, standing and helping his bride to her feet. She smiled at him adoringly as he pulled her close and kissed her softly.

They were certainly stronger than I was. How my brother had managed to not kiss Sarah until their wedding day, I'd never know, but I knew enough to know that I could never do that.

Though honestly, with my luck with guys, who knew the next time I'd have the opportunity to kiss one, anyway.

I'd thought I had the perfect man. Someone who supported me, believed in my photography, and would always be there for me. Turned out that not only was he my client's son, but he was a serial dater and a wedding crasher, who'd seen me at a different client's wedding and assumed I would be an easy mark. So, when his sister had gotten engaged, he'd convinced his parents to hire me for her wedding, allowing him the opportunity to ask me out. He thought photographers were rich and assumed I would fund his extravagant lifestyle, but when it became obvious that I couldn't be that for him, he dumped me.

I'd never date a man I met at a wedding ever again.

"What are you brooding about?" my younger sister Kathryn asked, threading her arm through mine as the music started for Keith and Sarah's first dance as husband and wife.

"Idiot exes."

"Oh yes, such a fun topic to think about at our brother's wedding."

I laughed. "Sorry, you're right. I'll stop."

We watched Keith twirl Sarah, both of them glowing like stars in the night sky.

"Do you think we'll ever be that happy?" Kat asked softly.

"Absolutely," I said, though I didn't believe it for myself. "You are amazing and some guy is going to adore you someday. And until then, we've got each other."

"What do we have each other for?" my best friend Natalie asked, plopping down into the chair on my other side.

"Being happy and ignoring our state of singleness," Kathryn said.

"Ah, yes. We can be happy spinsters together until someday when our true loves come riding in on white horses."

Our brother Kyle joined us, sitting down in Keith's empty chair next to Natalie. "Ashley is driving me up the wall," he muttered, so quietly I almost couldn't hear him.

Natalie gave him a sympathetic smile. "Weddings can make girlfriends act a little strange."

Ashley didn't need help acting strange–she had that handled on her own. She was probably jealous of Sarah, even though Sarah had left everything behind to come after my brother and wasn't an heiress any longer.

I wished Kyle would just break up with her and date someone better for him, someone who understood our family more.

Seeing him sitting next to Natalie while she listened to him complain about his girlfriend made me take a closer look at the two of them.

In the past two years I'd spent photographing weddings, I'd seen some couples with a lot less chemistry than my brother and my best friend, even though they weren't dating.

If they ever did date, whew, the sparks would fly.

"Having fun without me?" our youngest sister Krystal asked, dropping into the seat on Kathryn's other side.

"The gang's all here now," Kathryn said wryly.

My siblings, best friend, and I watched as Keith kissed his bride on the dance floor and released her to our father, who stepped forward to spin Sarah around the dance floor for the father-daughter dance. They may not have been biologically related, but our father had claimed Sarah as his own after her father disowned her, and she had blossomed with a family's love.

"Man, can you imagine what it's going to be like when all of us are married?" Krystal asked, wrinkling her nose.

I could imagine it. For everyone except me.

I saw dozens of couples on the happiest day of their lives. I knew what happiness in a relationship looked like, and I knew what my past relationships had looked like. They didn't look anything like the ones that worked out.

Maybe I just wasn't cut out for love.

I could be happy as the spinster Aunt Kait, spending all my time and money doting on my many nieces and nephews, documenting all of their family moments and watching my siblings live wonderful lives with their spouses.

Because after my last relationship, I doubted I would ever find that myself.

But for now, it was enough to join my siblings on the dance floor to celebrate Keith and Sarah, knowing that they had the kind of relationship that could stand the test of time.

**Will Kaitlyn get her happily ever after?
Find out in FALLING FOR HER CLIENT,
a Sweet Small Town Romance.**

*Hiring the girl of his dreams was supposed to bring them together,
but she has a rule: no dating the clients.*

After her last disastrous relationship, Kaitlyn Palmer has given up on love. She's ready to focus on growing her photography business and discovering herself, even if it's hard to ignore the jealousy that creeps in during every romantic photo session.

Cody Nolan had put love on the backburner for years, but he's finally ready to settle down. When he attends a charity fundraiser as a favor and wins a picnic basket date with Kaitlyn, he thinks she's smart, driven, and drop-dead gorgeous too. She's everything he's been searching for and more—and to make things even better, his hint-dropping mother will absolutely love her.

When their first interaction ends awkwardly, hiring Kaitlyn to photograph an event seems like the perfect excuse to see her again until he discovers that she has one rule: no dating the clients. Now, Cody has to dig deep to convince Kaitlyn he's worthy of a chance to prove he's better than the other men who've hurt her.

Thank you so much for reading FALLING FOR THE HEIRESS.
I hope you enjoyed it. If you did, please consider leaving a
review—it helps more than you know!

Want more of the Palmer family?
Sign up for the newsletter to learn more about the Palmer family
and get updates and bonus content!

https://gabriellelandi.com/newsletter

Find me online at:
GabrielleLandi.com
Facebook: Author Gabrielle Landi
Twitter: @LandiWrites
Instagram: @LandiWrites

About The Author

Gabrielle Landi lives in Southern Indiana with her husband and children and has a soft spot for every stray cat that ends up on her front porch. When she's not writing, she spends her time chasing children, wishing there was more coffee, and eating chocolate like it's her job. If she had to write her own love story in tropes, it would include second chance romance and a secret relationship, and would be entirely unbelievable.

Acknowledgments

When you have ten years of history behind a book, where do you begin?

First of all, thanks to all of the Twitter friends who have watched me grow from a baby writer to a published author. There are far too many of you to name, but your friendship, encouragement, and words of support mean more than you know.

To the ASoS group chat and Moms Who Write discord pals - thank you for cheerleading me through the last year of preparing to publish. This wouldn't have happened without you.

To those who had a hand in shaping this novel, from beta reading (Emily Thompson, Stephanie Allen, and Drea Laj), to editing (Julia Byers), proofreading (Elle Wilson), and more - you are all lifesavers and I appreciate you so much. Each of you made this novel better.

To my family:

My parents, siblings, grandparents, and in-laws - your support means the world to me. Thank you for always asking what I'm working on and how it's going. And thanks, Mom, for encouraging me to keep going, even after you read the awful first draft of that first novel, ten years ago. I hope you think this one is a lot better!

My kids - you make every day magical and I love seeing life through your eyes. Thank you for making me want to be a better person in every way. An extra shoutout to baby girl K, who made this novel even more challenging as I wrote, edited, and published it with her along for the ride, whether in the womb or strapped on with a baby carrier. We did it.

And finally, my husband. Thanks for inspiring all of my heroes in some way, and for always making me smile.

I love you all.